AINSLEY KEATON

The Beachfront Secrets

VINCI
BOOKS

By Ainsley Keaton

Sconset Beach

Vinci Books

vinci-books.com

Published by Vinci Books Ltd in 2025

1

Copyright © Ainsley Keaton 2022

The publisher and the author have made every effort to obtain permissions for any third party material used in this book and to comply with copyright law. Any queries in this respect should be brought to the attention of the publisher and any omissions will be corrected in future editions.

A CIP catalogue record for this book is available from the British Library.

Paperback ISBN: 9781036703738

Chapter One

Hallie

Late September

Hallie Gleason had been working with Willow at her spa for several months, and she'd just decided to become a life coach. She realized how much she loved seeing clients and helping them through their life challenges and knew she would love to do more of that. She was learning about integrative nutrition and was working for her online degree in that field. And Willow was able to help their clients through acupuncture, crystal and herbal therapies and, sometimes, sound therapy. She used Tibetan Singing bowls in different keys to unblock chakras and get energy flowing freely.

But sometimes, it seemed their clients needed a bit more therapy because they were making a mess of their lives, and Hallie went the extra mile to sit down with them and help them work through goals and challenges. She found she had a natural affinity for such a practice. She never knew she had it in her to hold somebody's hand and help them emotionally through a divorce, for instance, or help somebody overcome their mental blocks so they can believe in themselves enough to find a better job, as another instance.

So, Hallie went to Willow to ask her if that would be another avenue they might go into. Willow agreed that it was definitely something that would fit well with their wellness spa. "Sure, it would be going the extra mile for our clients," she agreed. "I can unblock their energies and help them feel better about life, in general, but people also need practical advice on going forward. You seem to really enjoy that type of thing, and you don't need to be certified to become a life coach, so why not? I think it would be an excellent addition to our practice."

Hallie smiled, and then Willow just suddenly stopped and looked at her. Hallie raised an eyebrow in question, but Willow just shook her head. "It's nothing, nothing," she said but then put her hand to her chest. "Have you seen a doctor lately?" she asked.

Hallie shook her head. "I'm embarrassed to admit, I haven't for a while. I suppose I'm overdue for getting my cholesterol checked and my hormones evaluated and whatnot." She was seeing an endocrinologist regularly before because her hormones were out of whack because of her menopause, and she was seeing a psychiatrist for her depression, but she hadn't seen a gynecologist in a long time for her usual Pap smear and breast exam. And she wasn't seeing her endocrinologist anymore because she was feeling so good that she stopped getting treatment for her menopause symptoms. The same thing for her psychiatrist.

Willow nodded her head. "See a doctor yesterday," she said. "Don't wait."

2

Hallie scrunched her eyebrows. This didn't sound good, to say the least. "Why?"

"Just see a doctor," she said. "A gyno. When was the last time you've done a breast exam on yourself?"

Hallie drew a breath. "I don't, I…" She trailed off, not wanting to admit she didn't do one on herself regularly at all, and she never did.

"Okay, dude, say no more. Seriously, you need to get better at taking care of yourself."

Hallie suddenly felt shy. "Do you see somebody regularly?" she tentatively asked Willow.

"Yeah," she said. "Every year, I get that damn metal speculum shoved up inside me. The doctor always says she warms it up, but it sure doesn't feel like it. And I get the breast exams with it at that time. I get a regular checkup every year as well, where I get bloodwork done and all that. I don't mess around with my health. Cancer runs in my family. Mom died of ovarian cancer, and my sister has had several cancer scares herself. Sybil, my sister, just gets benign cysts on her breasts, and she's had a few taken out surgically. And I've had a thing called cervical dysplasia that can turn into cancer if I'm not careful. So, yeah, I'm pretty up on my health."

Hallie suddenly felt a chill. "Willow, uh, is there any reason you're so adamant I see a doctor?"

She nodded her head. "Yeah. Something's wrong. I don't know what, but I can feel something is. Seriously, make an appointment and get yourself checked out. You'll thank me afterward, guaranteed."

Hallie shook her head. Things were going so well for her. She'd lived for many years in a miserable state - living within a failing marriage with a husband who couldn't care less about her. She didn't talk to her daughter Morgan because she smothered Morgan so much that Morgan needed to separate from her completely.

That all had changed in the past few years. She came to the island, found Willow and her special treatments, learned how to stand on her own two feet, came to terms with her daughter and generally found her joy. Surely there wasn't some other dark cloud that would devastate her. Was there?

As she looked into Willow's face, she knew.

Yes, there was something that would be a challenge for her.

And it was going to be her greatest challenge so far.

Chapter Two

Hallie

A few days after Willow gave Hallie her warning about her health, Hallie knew it was time to have an emergency meeting with the ladies. She'd made an appointment with a gynecologist at The Nantucket Cottage Hospital, but, unfortunately, she wouldn't be able to see that doctor for another two weeks.

And she was starting to panic just a little. It didn't help that Willow just shook her head when Hallie told her she couldn't see anybody for two weeks. "Dude, you shouldn't wait one more day, but you do you."

Hallie knew Willow was psychic. Everyone who knew her knew about her abilities. So, Willow wasn't just talking. She really meant there was something wrong, and Hallie was becoming more and more terrified. So, she needed her ladies to talk her down.

Ava was able to be there for Hallie more than ever before. She had a full-time employee, Jessica Bennett, staying with her at the inn. Jessica was basically a waif who needed Ava's guidance and love to help her through a very difficult time. In exchange for Ava's guidance, love and room and board, Jessica was helping out at the inn and doing a spectacular job of it.

Hallie was happy for Ava and even happier that Ava seemed genuinely content in her relationship with Deacon Cromwell, a much-younger handsome contractor whom Ava hired to renovate her house all those months ago. Ava was doing extremely well in her life, and Hallie couldn't be more thrilled.

Quinn, her other best friend, was also doing well. She had quite the shock when the girl she gave up for adoption literally showed up on her doorstep, and the two went through quite a rocky road together for a while. But things had smoothed out. Her daughter, Emerson, was now enrolled in school and was enjoying a normal 13-year-old girl's life of friends, homework, video games and playing her violin like a virtuoso.

As for Sarah, Ava's sister and Hallie's new friend, she seemed happy, too. She was working for Ava as a sommelier and living with Quinn for the time being. She was gathering her own thoughts and had spent the last few months in serious introspection and had emerged more content in her life than she'd ever felt. In fact, she said she had a bit of news of her own for everyone and Hallie was excited to find out what that news was.

Ava's life was also slowing down because it was late September. Therefore, her busy season was over. The island was winding down after hosting raucous carousing and partying over the summer months, when the population swelled to 50,000 when, during the slow season, it was only around 10,000. The crowds were gone, the traffic was becoming lighter, and Hallie felt she could breathe again.

The ladies met on Ava's terrace that evening. This was the first time in a while they could meet there because, during Ava's busy months, people were usually hanging out on her rooftop terrace. But now, her inn was only at 20% capacity, not 100%, and it was certainly much quieter around her house. That meant they could use the terrace sometimes, especially during the weekdays, for their meetings.

Hallie loved Ava's terrace. Her house looked out on the 'Sconset Beach, and you could hear the water rolling in at night when all was quiet. It was a lulling sound, relaxing and almost hypnotic. And so it was that evening - the beach below was quiet, deserted, and Hallie could hear the ocean clearly. It made her smile.

Hallie got to Ava's at 7, as did Quinn. Sarah was already on the terrace with Ava, drinking a glass of wine. Ava came over and gave Hallie a hug. "Dear, what's this about? You sounded stressed over the phone."

Hallie sat down, and Ava poured her a glass of wine. There was a spread of food already prepared and waiting on the table - veggie lasagna made at the inn, along with some garlic bread and a huge salad. Everybody sat down, helped themselves to the food, took their seats on lounge chairs, balanced the food on their laps, and sat their glasses of wine on side tables placed around the loungers.

Hallie drank her wine, ate her food, and wondered what to tell everyone. A part of her didn't want to say anything to anyone about it because, if she didn't say anything, maybe none of it would turn out to be real. And she didn't really know what was wrong with her, anyhow. Willow just urged her to see a doctor. That was all.

But that was enough, and Hallie knew it. If Willow was genuinely worried about something, then something was genuinely wrong. There was no getting around it.

She finally opened her mouth to speak. "Uh, I think something might be wrong with me. Physically."

"What do you mean?" Ava asked, her hand covering Hallie's.

"Willow, uh, as you know, she has a sixth sense that's completely on target."

Quinn smiled. "Don't I know that. I'll never forget how she helped me track down Emerson when that little rascal tried to escape back to Boston without telling anyone." Quinn referred to an incident where her little daughter Emerson got a wild hair and left the beach without notifying anyone. For a few hours, a frantic Quinn thought Emerson had been kidnapped. But Willow told Quinn that Emerson was heading to Boston on her own and was at the ferry dock. That's exactly where Quinn found her wayward daughter. This incident made Quinn a believer in Willow's abilities.

Ava dug into her lasagna and then pointed her fork at Quinn. "Yes, and she also set my mom straight. She knew my mom's secrets. She knew my mother had a female love and that the guy I always thought was my dad really wasn't. Don't ask me how she figures these things out, but she does, that's for sure."

"I know," Hallie said. "And that's what worries me." She took a deep breath. "She urged me to see a doctor. She told me not to delay. There's obviously a serious health issue that she's picking up on. And I'm really, really scared."

Ava put her hand on Hallie's, and Quinn did the same. Sarah came up behind her and wrapped her arms around her neck.

Nobody really knew what to say. Everyone knew that if Willow was worried, then Hallie was right to be scared.

"Hallie, whatever is wrong, we'll handle it together. When is your doctor's appointment?"

"In two weeks," Hallie said. "I'm going to be on pins and needles until then. I mean, what if-" She cut off that thought, not wanting to finish it. She didn't have to finish that thought, anyhow. Everyone knew just what was on her mind.

It was always a woman's biggest fear that a routine checkup would turn dark. It happened every day to millions of women. They go to a doctor and are told to return as soon as possible. Some test results don't quite look right, or maybe an x-ray shows a spot on a vital organ. The result of the colonoscopy is in, and there's an abnormality. On and on and on. Then more tests, more waiting, and then the grim news.

Hallie prayed she wouldn't be put through that gauntlet, although she imagined she would.

"I'll be with you at the doctor's," Ava quickly said. "Things are slower for me now, and Jessica has been a tremendous help. I can take as much time as you need me to take."

"Me, too," Sarah said.

"And me," Quinn said. "We'll all be there."

Hallie smiled at her ladies. "Thanks for all the support, but I'm not sure it's such a good idea for all of you ladies to be hanging around the waiting room. And the doctor's offices usually don't have room for more than one person. So…"

"We'll draw straws," Quinn said.

"No, we'll take turns," Sarah said. "Ava, you go with her on the first doctor's visit, and if there's a follow-up, God forbid, Quinn will go. And I'll go on the third one, and so on and so forth."

Hallie nodded. "That sounds like a good plan. Maybe I'll get lucky, and there will be only one visit. The doctor will give me a clean bill of health and send me on my way."

Everybody got quiet for a few moments, and Hallie started to feel uncomfortable in the silence. "Okay, Sarah, you have some news for us. Maybe your news is happier?"

Sarah smiled. "Maybe. I got something very mysterious in the mail. It's postmarked from France, which is weird. The only person I know in France is Nolan's ex-wife, Olivia. Anyhow, the envelope contained only one thing. A single penny."

"Oh?" Quinn said with a big grin on her face. "A mystery. I love that. Do you have that mystery penny on you by any chance?"

"Yeah, I do," Sarah said. And then she got up and got her purse and brought the penny out of it. "I can't figure out why she would send this to me. If it was Olivia who sent it, that is."

Olivia was the wife of Sarah's boyfriend, Nolan, who was a billionaire. Nolan never divorced Olivia, even though Olivia had long been living in the South of France with her longtime boyfriend, Gabriel. When Sarah and Nolan met, Olivia had already been living with Gabriel for three years.

Nolan tragically died of ALS, leaving Sarah penniless and Olivia the sole heir to his billions. Olivia had never even called Nolan even after the international papers had announced his diagnosis, and she didn't attend his funeral. Sarah had patiently nursed Nolan until his death, and she got nothing from his estate because he refused to make a will.

All that seemed patently unfair to all the ladies, but what could anybody do? The law was the law, and if somebody died without a will, their spouse gets their entire estate. And so it happened. But Sarah wasn't bitter about any of that. She just accepted it, put her head down, and made something of herself. She'd just gotten her Level 2 certification as a sommelier, making herself invaluable to Ava. But, now that Ava was experiencing the off-season, there was less need for Sarah, so Sarah was currently thinking about getting a job as a bartender for one of the upscale restaurants in town.

Now, she was the proud owner of a penny. Hallie had to wonder about that. A penny! Was Olivia trying to drive in yet another injustice onto Sarah's head? Wasn't it enough that Olivia got billions she didn't earn, when it should've been Sarah who was made instantly wealthy after Nolan's death?

Sarah showed the penny to everybody. "Looks like a penny," Ava said. "But it's weird. It's really old, but it looks brand new."

"I know," Sarah said. "That's what I was noticing. But so what? It's a brand-new looking old penny. Big whoop."

Hallie examined it. It was a 1943-D penny. It looked pretty ordinary.

She gave it back to Sarah. "Well, it wouldn't hurt to take this penny to a numismatic guy. You might have to go to Boston to do that, though. I don't think they have one on the island." Hallie's ex-husband was an avid coin collector, but Hallie knew little about the subject. She wished she could be a bigger help on the matter, but it was what it was.

Sarah drew a breath and rolled her eyes. "Yeah, I was afraid I would have to go off-island to find out what this thing means, if anything at all. But I have a gut feeling it's something significant. If Olivia sent it to me, it must mean something."

"Did you know her?" Ava asked.

"No," Sarah said. "Never met the woman in my life. I mean, I know of her, of course. Nolan used to talk about her all the time, none of it good. Who knows what the real story was between them? I get the feeling there was bad blood between Nolan and Olivia, though. And that's all I really know."

"Well, you know she never even called Nolan after it was known that he was dying. She gets papers in France, she gets the internet in France, everybody knew about his disease," Quinn said. "So, either that speaks to her character, or it speaks to Nolan's. And, from what you tell me about the man, I'd say the latter."

And that was true. Sarah had told the girls that when Nolan was diagnosed with his disease, it was a big story, just because of who his father was. His father was a prominent CEO of a large pharmaceutical company, and was worth billions. And, because ALS is relatively rare, the news picked up on the fact that Nolan was suffering from it. So, it was true. Olivia had to have known that Nolan was dying.

Sarah nodded her head. "Yes, he was a manipulative jerk. But not so much so that Olivia would've hated him. Again, I don't know what happened between them. What I do know is that she took his billions without question. So, I don't know why she would send me a penny unless she just wants to twist the knife for some odd reason."

Hallie knew something about waitressing, as she'd done it a few times. And leaving a penny on the table was considered the ultimate insult. For some odd reason, a shiny penny was more of an insult than a dull one. She was embarrassed to admit she had a few pennies left on tables in her time, which was because she was a terrible waitress, and she knew it.

So, the only thing that Hallie could think of was that Olivia was insulting Sarah for some reason. But she couldn't think of why. Sarah just said she didn't know Olivia, so why would she go out of her way to do this to her? That was the mystery.

Sarah just shrugged her shoulders. "Is it even worth going to a coin collector place? I mean, it's going to involve me going to Boston, and I'm just going to get into the place, and the guy's just going to laugh at me. And, presto, I'm out $400 for the round trip plane ticket, and I really can't afford it right now."

Ava nodded her head. "Sarah, you're going to Temecula next week. Why don't you drive a half-hour south to San Diego and find somebody there? Two birds, one stone."

Sarah touched her nose. "You're right. That's a really good idea. I mean, it's worth a shot, but it's not worth a special trip to find somebody to tell me this penny is just a penny. Well, we'll have to see how things go."

Hallie laughed. "Wouldn't it be great if that penny was some kind of rare coin that was worth millions of dollars?"

Sarah laughed as well. "Oh yeah, and I'm sure the next lottery ticket I buy will be the big jackpot! Just think, I can buy my own island!"

Ava got into the act. "Sarah, I know some guys who own their own island, and they're a bunch of jerks. You don't want to buy an island, trust me," she said with a laugh.

The ladies drank wine for the rest of the evening while

fantasizing about Sarah somehow hitting the jackpot with her little penny.

It was nice to talk about the penny because it took Hallie's mind off of the scary prospect that would happen for her in a couple of weeks.

Chapter Three

Charlotte

Charlotte Killeen leaned over and looked at the clock. It read 2 AM. The space next to her in her ginormous California King was empty. She knew how hard her husband, Matthew, worked. He was a *sous* chef at a five-star restaurant in town. He usually arrived home late, especially on a Saturday night, and this Saturday night was no exception.

She sighed and went into Siobhan's room. The little girl was just over a year old, and she was over her sleepless nights when Charlotte would have to go into her room every hour, on the hour, throughout the night, to check on her and feed her. Of course, she got no help from Matthew because Matthew worked 60 odd hours a week, and the last thing he wanted to deal with when he was home was dirty diapers and spit-up.

Siobhan was sleeping peacefully, her tiny hand in her mouth. Her legs twitched in her sleep, and her head nodded slightly. She looked like she was having a dream of some sort. Charlotte wondered if tiny babies like Siobhan actually did dream, or maybe the twitch was involuntary.

As she looked at the sleeping child, her thoughts drifted to her mother, Ava. Her mother was now living on Nantucket, and she was sure Ava had expected her to visit more often. And she had, a few times, but she didn't really like to.

She was a great disappointment to her mother. That much she knew. Not that she blamed her in the end. She got an expensive degree and she didn't use that degree even one day. Her mother had spent over $300,000 on her Ivy League education, and what did she have to show for it?

She started dating Matthew her junior year at Cornell, and the two married her senior year. She had every intention of attempting to find a job, even after Matthew got his first job as a pastry chef and inherited a house here in Boston. But fate dealt her a different hand, as she got pregnant with Siobhan right after graduation, which was a year after they got married.

Even after discovering she would have a baby, she wanted to get a job. She felt too guilty about all the money her mother outlaid for her degree not to at least try. But she found her degree was useless without her going further in schooling and getting at least a master's, preferably a Ph.D. She had dreams of becoming a museum curator when studying at NYU. But everywhere she looked, museums asked for a master's or 5 years experience. She looked into some arts-related non-profit organizations, but those jobs were also very much in demand. She had been beaten out for every job she looked into.

She ended up working as a salesperson in the Thomas Kinkade gallery in Boxford, about a half-hour away, because she couldn't find anything else. Then she had to bed rest for the final three months of her pregnancy, as she was diagnosed with preeclampsia, and she promptly lost her job. She inquired with her grandmother Colleen about whether she should file a lawsuit against the gallery. Grandma Colleen told her it would be more trouble than it was worth.

When the baby was born, the gallery asked her back, and she considered it. They told her they expected her to come back to work after Siobhan was three months old. She was breastfeeding at the time, but she looked into breast pumps and thought she could try to make it work.

However, after being home with Siobhan for three months, Charlotte couldn't imagine trying to raise her while working full time. She wasn't making that much money at the gallery, anyhow. She was just a salesperson, working on commission. Daycare was extraordinarily high, and, combined with expenses for the wear and tear on her car and gas and time spent on the daily commute, it just wasn't worth it to keep working.

She didn't want to admit to her mother that she wasn't working because she had failed to find a lucrative position, even though she had tried her hardest. So, she told her mother that she was staying at home with Siobhan because that was what she had chosen for herself.

Her mother didn't say as much, but Charlotte knew Ava disapproved of her decision to not work outside the home. Her mother was all about independence and always told her she needed to not depend on anybody, certainly not a man, for financial decisions.

"What happens if something happens to Matthew?" Ava had asked.

"We have life insurance," Charlotte replied.

"I mean, what happens if he leaves you?" Ava countered.

"Well, I'll get half of-"

"Half of what? Matthew inherited that house, so that's considered his separate property if you guys divorce. You'll only be entitled to half of the amount that property increased over your marriage, and you've only been married for not even two years."

Charlotte had sighed when she got that lecture, again. The truth was, if she and Matthew divorced, she would end up with nothing. Considering Matthew's income, child support would be less than $300 a week, so she really was living on a precipice.

And she increasingly felt like she was about to fall off that precipice.

Siobhan continued to sleep while Charlotte sat in a rocking chair, staring at her child. She loved the little girl, but, she had to admit, she wasn't exactly ready for her, or for any other child, for that matter. She was happy about her, but her husband, Matthew, was decidedly not.

Before they married, Matthew told Charlotte he wasn't interested in having children, and Charlotte agreed with him at the time. She envisioned herself working in a glamorous career, maybe surrounded by high-profile celebrities while she helped open a gallery for a hip, up-and-coming artist. She would be the host of the most fabulous parties on the East Coast.

That was her hope. Of course, life never quite turns out the way one hopes. You make plans, and God laughs.

Siobhan was a surprise, but really, she shouldn't have been. Charlotte had secretly stopped taking the pill for over a year before becoming pregnant. She wasn't trying to trick her husband, but she didn't like how the pill made her feel.

It made her bloated, gave her migraines, and her mood swings were out of control. So, she just stopped. And started playing Russian Roulette.

For an entire year, she didn't get the bullet. She carefully tracked her cycle, using the rhythm method. On days when her calendar showed she was ovulating, she would tell Matthew she wasn't feeling well, so she couldn't make love.

That worked. For an entire year, that worked. And then, out of the blue, it didn't work.

Looking back, it was inevitable she would eventually get pregnant, but she never wanted to think of that. The rhythm method was only 80% effective, so she always had a good chance of getting pregnant. She told herself, however, that it was safe. Nothing was going to happen. She only had a 20% chance of getting pregnant if she was careful with her schedule, which she was.

She thought about how he reacted very negatively when she told Matthew about the pregnancy. He told Charlotte he didn't want a family. He wanted it to be the two of them and their friends. He told her he expected her to be able to take off at a moment's notice to go to Italy with him because his job had informed him that he would have to travel overseas from time to time to learn from some of the chefs over there when new European pastries and desserts were introduced in the restaurant. He told her he wanted his freedom to go wherever he pleased, whenever he pleased, be it to the movies or out to eat, and he wanted her to go along with him.

She got a lump in her throat as she watched Siobhan, wondering if she made a mistake in marrying Matthew. Or maybe she made a mistake in keeping Siobhan? She would never have thought about having an abortion. That just wasn't in her. She was pro-choice, but only for other people.

For herself, she simply couldn't have chosen that route. She'd discussed putting Siobhan up for adoption with Matthew, which was actually the way he wanted to go.

"I know it will be hard for you," Matthew had said to her. "Going through your pregnancy, then having to give her up. But that would be best for us."

At the time, Charlotte agreed. But she hedged, saying she didn't want to decide until after the baby was born. However, after Charlotte told Matthew she was considering putting Siobhan up for adoption, Matthew really liked the idea and started to fixate on it. He talked about it all the time, as if it was a done deal.

"I got in touch with an adoption agency, and they're very anxious to meet with us. They have parents all lined up for the baby. She'll have a good home," he would say to Charlotte.

Charlotte felt as if Matthew was talking about giving up a naughty puppy, the way he so cavalierly spoke about their child "going to a good home." As if, after the baby was born, the two of them were going to take the child down to the animal shelter and hope for the best.

"That's nice," Charlotte would say.

Then Matthew started bringing home files of prospective parents who would be interested in their baby. "This couple, Rory and Susan Cornwell, would be ideal. Rory is a structural engineer working with the federal government, so he's set. Susan is a kindergarten teacher and is looking forward to being a stay-at-home mother. They have a beautiful house in Roanoke, Virginia, acres of land and horses. I don't think we could find a more ideal home for our baby."

Somehow, the more Matthew talked about it, the more sour Charlotte felt about the adoption idea. He never even noticed that Charlotte wasn't as into the idea as he was. He never questioned why he was doing all the work, finding prospective parents, talking to adoption counselors and doing background checks, while Charlotte did nothing at all to help the adoption idea along. To her, it was only an idea, one she wished she'd never verbalized.

It was actually an idea she only presented to Matthew because she wanted him to shoot it down. She wanted him to say, "don't be silly. We aren't going to do anything of the sort. That baby is our baby. I love you, and I will love the baby, too." And then he was going to kiss her and tell her she was being crazy, and he suddenly realized, after Charlotte said that adoption was an option, how much he was just dying to start their family together.

But that wasn't his reaction to her adoption idea. His reaction was, "thank God you're saying this. I've been thinking about nothing else myself. We're finally on the same page."

Siobhan finally stirred as Charlotte realized it was 6 AM, and she'd been sitting in the room, staring at her daughter for four hours. The baby smiled at Charlotte, cooed and kicked her little legs. She was such a happy baby, Charlotte thought. She changed her diaper, realizing Matthew still wasn't home from his job.

Of course, he wasn't home. In the back of her mind, she knew why. The restaurant closed at 9 PM, and there was clean-up work to do afterward. Matthew also stayed after hours, planning the menu, working on recipes and talking to the top chefs. The restaurant was less than a half-hour away.

So, when she woke up in the middle of the night, at 2 AM, and saw Matthew's side of the bed was empty, and she assumed he was still at work, she was lying to herself. She knew in her heart he wasn't working that late.

She couldn't deal with the truth. Couldn't face it. Matthew had pulled away from her completely after Siobhan was born. At Siobhan's birth, he was at her bedside with a young couple he had been in contact with. Deborah and Richard Fields were anxious to arrange a private adoption with their baby. Matthew had desperately tried to make Charlotte sign her parental rights over to the couple.

"They're progressive, cultured, educated, and they live in Boston in a beautiful brownstone. All you have to do is sign these papers terminating your parental rights, and the little baby can go home with them. Just think, the little girl can grow up in Beacon Hill in a historic building, surrounded by hip and progressive people."

She loved Beacon Hill, but that didn't mean she wanted her daughter to grow up there. "The baby's name is Siobhan," she told her husband. "She's our baby. And she will stay our baby."

It was then that the nurse brought the little girl to her. She hadn't laid eyes on her before that, apparently because Matthew had already told the nurse and doctors that the baby would go to adoptive parents. Therefore, it wasn't advisable for Charlotte to see her.

She looked into the little girl's eyes, seeing that the baby was born with red curls. Her button nose and round face looked just like her own mother's. She looked at Siobhan, saw Ava, and chuckled. "Figures," she said. "The baby is a little throwback." She covered the baby's head with the blanket, inhaled her scent and kissed her lightly on the forehead.

Then she stared right at Matthew. "Our baby," she said firmly. She didn't waver this time. Didn't try to appease him. Didn't even hint she would change her mind. "I will not sign those papers. Please take them someplace and shred them. Now."

Things had been strained between them ever since.

And now this. He just stopped coming home. He stopped pretending he was her husband. She stopped pretending he was Siobhan's father.

Everybody was pretending before. She created a reality where Matthew would fall in love with Siobhan and agree to become a family. Matthew created a reality where Siobhan would go to a "good home" somewhere in Roanoke, Virginia or in Beacon Hill. Then it would be just the two of them. They could go to the Bahamas, go to Europe, take a river cruise down the Rhine or the Danube, hike the Alps, or explore Italy's wine country. All things they had discussed doing before they were married.

Neither Matthew nor Charlotte saw their desired reality manifest, and it was tearing them apart.

Chapter Four

Charlotte

Matthew finally arrived home that evening. He had been gone for more than 24 hours, the longest stretch he had stayed away.

By the time he stepped through the door, Charlotte was loaded for bear. She had had a particularly bad day, as Siobhan had spiked a fever and started throwing up, which meant a trip to Urgent Care, which, in turn, meant waiting for two hours in a crowded waiting room around people suffering from various degrees of sickness themselves.

By the time he came in the door at 7 PM that evening, Charlotte was finishing her third load of laundry for the day. Siobhan was throwing up so much that she was going through her clothing like wildfire, and, to top it off, she had been screaming non-stop that entire day. Charlotte was trying to balance Siobhan with her left arm while changing the laundry from the washer to the dryer with her right arm, which was a delicate balancing act. Still, it had to be done because Siobhan was out of clothes.

Matthew didn't even attempt to help her. Didn't try to take Siobhan off her hands or ask her if there was anything he could do to help. Didn't go into the kitchen to put the dirty dishes piled up in the sink into the dishwasher, let alone put the clean dishes away. Didn't try to apologize for being away for so long.

She was losing her mind at that point. Matthew's cold reception after being gone for so long was the last straw, and she still had a screaming child on her hands.

She would have to have it out with him, right at that moment and not a moment longer. But, with a screaming, puking child to deal with, there was just no way she could ever talk to Matthew straight. Still, she was going to have to try.

"Matthew, we need to talk," Charlotte said while she valiantly and futilely tried to balance Siobhan on her right shoulder. By that point, the baby's face was beet red, and she was screaming at the top of her lungs.

"What's wrong with her?" Matthew asked in a tone that was clearly not sympathetic.

"She has an ear infection. The doctor prescribed antibiotics, but those don't start working right away. So, she's been puking and crying all day."

"Puking? Why puking? I got ear infections when I was a kid, and I didn't puke. In fact, I ruptured my eardrums when I was a kid, and I still didn't puke." He shook his head.

"Babies sometimes puke with ear infections because it messes with their equilibrium and makes them sick," Charlotte said, rapidly losing patience with her husband. "And I would've loved to have you home here to help me with her."

Matthew raised his eyebrows. "I'm here now," he said as he calmly got up, got a hand towel, and soaked it in hot water. He heated up some olive oil. Then he came back into the living room. "Give me the baby."

Charlotte handed him Siobhan, who continued to scream. Charlotte was screaming louder than Siobhan inside her head, but she was screaming for many different reasons. She was screaming in frustration. She was screaming in grief about her life. She was screaming because she felt trapped, both by her own poor decisions and by her marriage.

Matthew calmly put the warm towels on the baby's ears and then put some warm olive oil into the ear canals. "I used to get a lot of ear infections when I was a kid, and this is what my mom did for me. She used sweet oil, but olive oil works just as well."

To Charlotte's surprise, Siobhan calmed down within a couple of minutes. And, because the child had not had a nap that day, she was obviously very tired. A few minutes later, Siobhan's eyes were closed.

Charlotte felt her blood pressure come down as Matthew calmly handed her the baby. "Put her down, and we'll talk," he said.

Charlotte put Siobhan into her crib and then went out to talk to Matthew.

"Thank God we're finally alone," Matthew said.

Charlotte felt her defensive hackles rise when he said that. "What's that supposed to mean? 'Thank God we're alone.' What, you don't want our daughter around?"

Matthew looked her right in the eye. "There you go again, putting words into my mouth." He shook his head. "Why do you have to take everything I say and twist it around? I meant, thank God we're alone because I need to talk to you, too."

Charlotte wasn't appeased and felt attacked. "Where have you been for the past 24 hours?"

"Not at work," he said. "I lost my job."

Charlotte shook her head. "I'm sorry?"

"I lost my job," Matthew said. "The restaurant is making budget cuts, and the last one hired is the first one fired. They gave me my notice two weeks ago. Yesterday was my last day."

"And you didn't tell me?"

Matthew just shrugged. "There was never a good time. I've been spending the last couple of weeks after hours at the hotel, in their business center, polishing my resume and looking at Zip Recruiter and Monster for a new job. Been working my contacts, too. Something will come up."

The restaurant that Matthew worked at was part of an upscale hotel, which was what he was referring to when he talked about spending time in the hotel.

"Something will come up? Something will come up? I'm sorry?"

Matthew took a deep breath. "Charlotte, we're going to lose this house. There's no money for the mortgage. Or, at least, there won't be in a few months. Things are tight out there right now. We're going to have to downsize."

Matthew had inherited the house, but the two had taken out a mortgage against it. This was yet another bone of contention between them because Matthew resented having to borrow against the house. As he saw it, Charlotte should've been working full time, and there shouldn't have been a baby around, so the couple wouldn't have the financial problems they had if Charlotte had given Siobhan up for adoption like he wanted.

Charlotte couldn't believe how cavalier he was being. "Matthew, what do you mean, we're going to lose this house?"

"I mean exactly that. You were the one who made the decision not to work and give us another mouth to feed. That was all you. If you would've gone with the plan you and I agreed to before we married, none of this would be happening. We would both have a good full-time income and no added expense of a baby."

"Oh, no, you're not going to put this on me." Charlotte shook her head rapidly. "That's not fair."

"Oh, isn't it? Isn't it fair?" Matthew stood up and started to pace. "We agreed, Charlotte. We agreed. We both would be working, not just me. There would be no children. We would be just us, making our way in the world together. With both of us working, there would be extra money to do all kinds of things. Do you remember us talking about seeing the world? Do you remember us talking about buying an Airstream camper that we could just take anywhere we wanted, anytime we wanted? Do you remember any of that?"

"Well, things changed," Charlotte said.

"Yeah, and, guess what? I didn't agree with things changing. I feel like you pulled a dirty trick on me, Charlotte."

Charlotte couldn't quite grasp what she was hearing. "*I* pulled a dirty trick? *I* pulled a dirty trick? What about *you*?"

"What about me?"

"You're having an affair." Charlotte crossed her arms in front of her and glared at him. "Admit it."

"No, Charlotte, I'm not. You can take that to the bank.

I've never lied to you before, and I don't plan on lying to you now."

"Then where were you for the past 24 hours?" she demanded. "If you aren't having an affair? And, by the way, I'm going to call BS on you not lying. You lost your job and didn't tell me."

"Right. I didn't lie to you, though. I just didn't tell you. There's a difference between actively lying and omitting."

Charlotte was quite sure her attorney mother and her judge grandmother would agree there was a difference between lies and omissions, but, to her, it was a distinction without a difference.

"It's the same thing!" she yelled.

"No, it's not. If you would've asked me if I lost my job, and I said 'no,' that would be lying. As it was, I was just omitting. Ask your mom if there's a difference between those two things. She'll tell you."

Charlotte felt steam coming out of her ears. "I'm not talking about a legal difference between terms. In effect, a lie and an omission are the same thing. We aren't going to agree about this, and we've gotten off track. I asked you where you were for the past 24 hours."

"I was over at David's," he said. "He had a party last night, and I went there after work. We were up until 4 AM, just talking to all the guys, having a good time. Then I slept late, we got some brunch at 2 and went sailing." He smiled and raised his arms out in front of him. "And here I am."

Sailing. Sailing. She'd spent the past 8 hours dealing with a puking, screaming child, and he was sailing. How dare he!

Charlotte raised her eyebrows. "Davie? David? Isn't that your single friend?"

"Yes, yes, it is. In fact, all my friends are single. Some of them have girlfriends, but none of them have kids. I mean, Charlotte, I'm 24 years old. So are you. We aren't at the time in our lives where we're supposed to be raising kids. We're at the time of our lives when we're supposed to be staying out late with our friends, having brunch with these same friends and going sailing on a Sunday afternoon. Sam and the guys are going to upstate New York next weekend to go wine-tasting, and I will be there with them for that, too."

Charlotte shook her head. "No, you're not. You're going to be right here, helping out with Siobhan and helping out around the house. If you lost your job, you need to find a new one, but on the weekends, you'll be around here."

Matthew just shook his head. "No, I'm not. Listen, Charlotte, if you would've just kept your end of the bargain, we would be winery-hopping together. Some of the guys in our group are bringing their girlfriends. We're all going to rent a house there for the weekend. If you had kept your word, you would be coming along. Now, you can't keep me here. You can't expect me to drop my friends and stop me from living the life I'm supposed to be living when I'm young like this. I'm sorry, you changed the formula, and you did it all on your own. You made a major decision on your own, so I'm going to make decisions on my own. And I'm going to live the life I should be living at my age."

Charlotte started to hyperventilate. "Where does this leave me? Where does this leave Siobhan? Where does this leave us? We're going to have to move from this place because you want to live the life of a single guy. What's going to happen to us?"

Matthew's expression softened. "Char, I love you. But I can't stop thinking about how we were when we met. Before Siobhan. Do you remember? All those lazy Sundays when we ate all our meals in bed? All those blissful nights when we would walk through New York City, holding hands and looking at the sights? All those rooftop dinners and that crazy weekend in the Hamptons with Jeff and that bunch? You were so much fun, Charlotte. We had such dreams. We talked about training for a marathon together, do you remember? Do you remember spending one entire weekend reading websites about European river cruises, plotting out every stop? Not once, during all our all-night talking sessions, did we mention the word 'child.' Not once."

Charlotte shook her head. "Well, Siobhan happened. She happened. It wasn't my fault. I know you don't believe that, but it wasn't. I took the pill, and I never missed even one." She was lying to him about that, of course, but she felt she had no choice but to keep on lying about it. If he knew the truth about her birth control method, that would be it. He could never forgive her. So, she felt she had no choice but to keep up the charade.

"I believe you," Matthew said, coming over to Charlotte and putting his arms around her. She laid her face in his chest and sobbed. "I believe you when you say you did everything right. These things happen sometimes. But Charlotte, you had a chance to give her up. You had a chance to make things right, and you didn't. Now, I feel trapped. Suffocated. I just want to live life the way I thought I would all along. I love you, but I need out."

It was Charlotte's turn to throw up at that point. "Excuse me," she said and then ran into the bathroom and hurled. Matthew was right behind her. He knelt down next to her, offering her a glass of water as he soothingly rubbed her back. She accepted his kindness, feeling confused. He just told her he wanted out of their marriage, yet, here he was, offering her comfort. Who was he?

She swallowed hard. "I have to go," she said. "I have to get out of here."

"I know," Matthew said. "We're going to have to sell this house. And then I think we need to live apart for a while. I don't know. Maybe I just need to sow my oats. I mean, not see other women or anything like that, but just have my freedom. Maybe when I'm on my own and I have my space, I'll see things differently. I can't guarantee anything. But all I can tell you is I'm not happy. I feel like I'm underwater. I need to come up for air. I need to come up for air."

———

That night, Charlotte packed her bags. She couldn't be in that house a moment longer. She didn't know where she would end up, but she knew where she was going to be soon.

Her mother's 'Sconset Inn'.

Chapter Five

Ava

Ava and Deacon were enjoying the day on the terrace, but Ava knew the conversation would soon turn dark. Ava had a great relationship with her handsome young contractor boyfriend. They enjoyed each other's company very much. They always had lots to talk about, and they had the same sense of humor, so they found the same comedies hilarious. And things physically were going very well, to Ava's surprise. She thought she was done with that part of her life, but she found out she wasn't, and that was a thrill.

But she would have to tell Deacon about Hallie. Ever since Hallie had her meeting with everybody, Ava had not been able to sleep because she was so worried about her. Yes, nothing was confirmed because Hallie could not see a doctor yet. At the same time, everybody knew Willow and how on point she always was with everything. The fact that she was that worried about Hallie gave Ava a chill.

"So, mate, what did you say you wanted to talk to me about?" he asked.

Ava explained about Hallie, and Deacon listened.

"Now, don't get over your skis, like you Americans might say. Or is the right expression cart before the horse? I have problems with these weird sayings. Anyhow, wait until she actually sees a doctor before you get worried. Then, if the doctor says she's sick, we'll deal with it. Don't forget, my sister had a deadly cancer, but she's just fine. Hopefully, Hallie will be too."

Ava took a deep breath and then was surprised. Her son, Jackson, was coming out to the terrace. Jackson was an actor out in Los Angeles, so Ava rarely saw him, but he tried to pop in as much as possible.

Ava got up and gave her son a big hug. "Jackson! What are you doing here? I mean, it's so good to see you, but I wasn't expecting you."

"I had a break in my schedule, so I decided to come out here in the future. Then Charlotte called me and asked me to come out here now, for some reason. She's supposed to meet me here. Is she here yet?"

Ava was confused. "No. Why, why is she coming here?"

"She has something to tell you, and she wanted to tell you in person because she didn't want to panic you over the phone."

That didn't sound good. Not in the least. "What does she want to tell me?"

"Not sure. It just sounds bad, whatever it is. Bad enough that she wanted me to be around. Funny she didn't call Samantha, though. After all, Sam lives here, doesn't she now?"

"Of course. You know that."

Samantha was working for a bakery in town, making wedding cakes. She had been really busy making one cake after another during the summer for many prestigious island weddings. She was extremely artistic and talented with cake-making, which was a relief to Ava because Sam was just lost in her life before she found her niche with the wedding cake thing. She was also extremely happy with her boyfriend, Grayson. Ava had a feeling Samantha was going to make it official with Grayson soon because Grayson had talked to Ava about it several times.

No doubt about it, Samantha was in a really good place. But unfortunately, Samantha and Charlotte never really got along that well. Charlotte and Jackson were always much closer than Charlotte and Samantha, which Ava didn't really understand. She thought sisters should be closer to one another than a sister and a brother, but that wasn't how it worked with her triplets. Charlotte looked up to Jackson, and she always did. She looked down on Samantha, Ava felt, so maybe that's what it was.

Of course, Charlotte didn't have a reason to look down on Samantha, even when Samantha messed up her life. And she really didn't have a reason to look down on her now, yet, she probably still did. At least, according to what Samantha said about her relationship with Charlotte, Charlotte still did see Samantha as being nothing but a screwup. Which wasn't fair, but it was what it was.

Ava looked at Deacon with concern. What now? Was Charlotte going to give her one more reason to worry? Probably. Having kids was like playing whack-a-mole. When you hit one mole, another one pops up, and you can never hit all the moles. Samantha was messing up in her life, and now she was good, so now it was time for Charlotte to mess up. Jackson would probably get his turn soon enough. Ava was only grateful her kids didn't have major crises at the same time.

Charlotte appeared on the terrace with Siobhan in her portable car seat. She looked at Jackson. "Thanks for coming. Mom, I need to talk to you about staying here. Me and Siobhan."

Ava shook her head. Thank goodness it was not her busy season anymore, and she was only at 50% capacity on any given day. Charlotte and Siobhan could have their own rooms in her house.

She should've been more surprised that Charlotte needed to move in with her. But she wasn't. She had a weird feeling for a while that something was not quite right with Charlotte and her husband. It was a mother's intuition. So, she had been bracing for this news for a few years. Now, here it was. Charlotte was apparently leaving her husband.

"You've come at a good time," Ava said. "I have the room, now. A month ago, I would've had to turn you down. But, tell me, what's going on?"

"Jackson, can we go down to the beach and talk? I really need to talk to a guy about this. No offense, mom, but I need a man's perspective on what happened between my husband and me."

Ava nodded her head. "Go talk to your brother. I'll be watching your daughter."

Deacon smiled. "And, me. If you need anybody to help you move, I'm your man."

Jackson shook his head. "And, I now know why Charlotte wanted me to be here so badly. She's going to need manpower to move."

"Well, that's part of it," Charlotte admitted. "But I also

need to talk to you about everything. I need to know that I'm not screwing up as badly as I think I am. Oh, Jackson, I just don't know what to do."

Jackson and Charlotte then disappeared to walk down to the beach.

Chapter Six

Charlotte

"Okay, sis," Jackson said as he and Charlotte walked along the beach. It was a clear and cool day, and the sounds of the waves were relentless and comforting to Charlotte. She tried to think that what had happened with Matthew was fixable, but, somehow, she couldn't think her way around it. "Now, what happened with your hubby?"

Charlotte sighed. "He doesn't want the baby," she said.

"No, shit, Charlotte. That's always been the case. What's changed?"

Charlotte sighed. "I mean-"

"Listen, Char, I love you. But you kinda broke your agreement with the dude. He thought he was marrying an independent woman who wanted to share his adventures. Instead, he ended up with an insta-family. That has to be whiplash-inducing to anybody. He probably needs time to process it."

Charlotte swallowed hard. "Who's side are you on?" she asked him.

"Nobody's side. Nobody's side. You told me that you wanted a guy's perspective on all this, so that's what I'm giving you."

Charlotte knew he was right. She *did* want his opinion. But only if his opinion agreed with her own. "So, what are you saying? Are you saying we're doomed?"

"No, not at all," Jackson said. "Doomed is such a loaded word. I'm saying that you need to give him his space. Let him figure out on his own what he wants. Let him live life the way he thinks he wants, and maybe he'll come around. But one thing's for sure - if you try to force the guy into doing what you want, he'll run far and fast. You know all those guys who go out for a pack of cigarettes and never come back home? They do that because they reach the end of their rope, and they've had enough. They do that because nobody is hearing them, and nobody will hear them. They do that because they literally can't breathe."

Charlotte was somewhat surprised to hear her brother say these things. She always assumed that men who abandoned their families were cowards and jerks.

"I don't agree with what you're saying," Charlotte said. "I think men who take off like that just can't handle the heat. They're weak, and they're cowardly. They're not real men. Real men are there for their wives and children and provide for their families. Real men don't kick their wife out just because she had his child."

She realized she was raising her voice, partly because the sound of the surf was so loud and partly because she was getting upset with her brother.

Why was she upset with Jackson? She knew him. He was her triplet brother. The two had an almost psychic connection shared between two people who shared a womb and grew up together, side by side. And he was never one to snow her. He always told it like it was. It was just that he had a perspective that Charlotte simply couldn't see.

Why couldn't he see that Matthew was just a bad guy?

Why wasn't he offering to beat Matthew up for her?

Jackson shrugged as he rolled up his jeans and waded further into the surf. He stood there on the shore with the waves lapping around his ankles and breathed in the salty air.

"Do you remember the first time you saw an ocean wave? Did you get as excited as I did when you saw your first palm tree? I'd only ever seen palm trees on T.V. before I moved to L.A. I somehow believed they didn't exist. Now, I see them all the time. They're a dime a dozen out in L.A. Do you remember the first time you saw a seal just lazing around on the beach?"

Charlotte shook her head. "I don't know what you're talking about. What does that have to do with what's going on with Matthew and me?"

"If you don't know what I'm talking about, then I'm not surprised you and Matthew are having issues." He walked further along, picking up seashells along the way. He tossed a big stick into the surf and smiled when he saw a dog come out of nowhere and chase after it. The dog brought it back, and a young girl called for it. The dog took off to where his mistress was, the branch in its jaws.

"Will you stop talking in riddles?" Charlotte asked Jackson. "What does any of that have to do with the problems between Matthew and me?"

Jackson put his arm around Charlotte as the two walked in the surf. "There are two kinds of people in the world. Those who appreciate the little things and those who don't see them. You're so focused on your own little world and being right that nothing else penetrates. Everybody has to see things your way, and if they don't, they're wrong. In the meantime, life passes you by. You aren't happy because you can't slip off the blinders."

Charlotte opened her mouth and then shut it again. "Are you saying Matthew and I would be having problems even if there was never a baby?"

"Maybe," Jackson said. "One thing's for sure, though. A baby will show the cracks sooner than they would've appeared if there wasn't a baby. There would've been cracks that would've shown up, sooner or later, in your marriage. But the two of you could have gone along without those cracks showing for years if Siobhan never came along."

Charlotte shook her head. "That's not true. Matthew told me I used to be fun. He reminded me that we shared a common dream of living life to the fullest. We were going to do things like hike in the mountains, go on rafting trips, take river cruises to European cities and ski in the Alps. I would do all of that with him, and he's mad we can't do those things now. We would've never had any cracks if not for Siobhan."

"Char," Jackson said. "Since when are you the outdoorsy, adventurous type? You always complained whenever mom took us camping growing up. You hated the bathrooms, the bugs, sleeping on the ground, the smells, the people in the next campsite, eating outdoors, the sounds of crickets outside. You hated that you didn't get Wi-Fi service out in the middle of nowhere. You always told mom that if we didn't stay in motels the whole way, instead of camping out, you would refuse to go on any more trips. There's nothing wrong with that, but none of that screams 'hiking in the mountains' and 'whitewater rafting' to me."

"Well, I was going to go hiking," Charlotte said. "I was going to do it for him."

"I'm calling B.S.," Jackson said. "You might've talked a good game of wanting to go hiking and rafting, but if he ever planned a trip, you would've made excuses about why you didn't want to go."

Charlotte knew Jackson was right. In fact, Matthew had planned a couple of hiking trips before Siobhan was born, and she *did* find excuses not to go. Then she got pregnant, which was her built-in excuse not to do anything she wasn't feeling - like hiking and rafting.

"And you're afraid of heights, right? You hate the snow, and you hate the cold. You don't like being wet, and you don't like falling down."

"Yes, and?"

"And you want to go skiing with Matthew?"

Charlotte was quiet. He put up a mirror to her face, and she didn't like it.

"And what do you say after a day at the beach?" Jackson asked.

"I complain about the heat, the sand getting every-where, my car getting too sandy, and how cold the water is." Charlotte knew all this was true. She and Matthew would occasionally go to Cape Cod to spend the day at the beach, and she hated it. She never understood the appeal of the beach. She couldn't get in the water because it was too cold. Well, it was too cold for her, not for other people. She'd inevitably miss putting sunscreen on a spot or two on her body, and she'd burn in these spots. Her scalp would burn because she usually forgot to bring a hat.

"Right," Jackson said. "And Matthew loves the beach, right? He loves to surf, doesn't he?"

"Sure," Charlotte said.

"And if he went to the beach and surfed without you, what would you say?"

"I'd complain. He should spend them with us on his days off, not surfing and playing around."

"Yet you probably wouldn't actually go to the beach with him if he asked, would you? Because you hate it?"

"Right," Charlotte said. "On his days off, he shouldn't want to play. He has things to do."

"You see the problem?" Jackson asked. "You're demanding he live in your world and only your world. You demand that he see things the way you see them, and if he sees them differently, he's wrong."

Despite herself, she felt her defensive hackles rise. "So I drove him away, is that what you're saying? I'm a horrible, bad person for keeping him from playing his life away. I shouldn't expect he'd want to stay home once in a while and care for his wife and child. Is that what you're saying?"

"There you go, putting words in my mouth," Jackson said. "I'm simply saying that you're trying to fit a square peg in a round hole. You're trying to tell a guy who wants to be out in the world doing things that he can't do anything that makes him happy. You think he's doing his duty. He sees a life of drudgery and nothing but. He sees that there will be only two things for him, work and work. Working outside the home, earning a living, and then coming home and working some more."

"Well, that's what adults do," Charlotte protested. "They realize life isn't all play. They don't shirk responsibility. They embrace it. They love raising their children and want to provide for their families. They feel fortunate to have a family to raise. A healthy baby and a loving wife are the only things he should need."

Jackson just nodded his head. "Okay. You're right. Now, let's get back up to the house."

Charlotte didn't say anything. She was ruminating over Jackson's words. Was he right? Did she expect Matthew just to bend to everything she wanted? Did she really not think about his needs at all? Was that why Matthew was pulling away? Was she throwing her marriage away because she was too rigid?

If Jackson was right, could she change?

She'd never be the girl Matthew wanted. The girl that she pretended to be when they were dating. And she was going to have a hard time letting Matthew play when he should be home with her. Whenever he told her he wanted to go surfing on his days off, she'd always pitched a fit and prevented him from doing so. She never willingly let him hang out with his friends - his friends were single. Nothing good could come from him hanging out with them. She prevented him from doing anything but work.

She thought she was doing the right thing. She needed help with Siobhan and help around the house. She needed to spend time with him. His free hours were limited, and she felt he should want to spend them with her.

Was she a ball and chain?

Maybe.

She was going to have to think about that one later.

Chapter Seven

Charlotte

That evening, after Charlotte had her talk with her brother, it was time to talk to Ava about what she needed from her. And it was time to get her mother's perspective on all of it.

She met her mom that evening on the terrace of the house. It was a calm evening, and the moon was full. The ocean sounds below were relaxing and lulled Charlotte's heart rate, which was beating fast before getting to the deck and gradually lowered with every wave that hit the shore.

That night, she explained everything to her mom. She told Ava the truth about the birth control situation. She knew by her mom's reaction to that news - she didn't seem surprised - that Samantha probably had already spilled the beans about that to her. Not that that surprised her. Samantha always did have a big mouth. Still, it was something that she told Samantha in confidence, and she was irritated with her sister.

After Charlotte told her mother about the birth control

situation, Ava simply nodded her head, took a sip of her wine, and asked Charlotte to go on with the story.

Charlotte told her all about the big fight she had with her husband. She told her about how Matthew had wanted to put Siobhan up for adoption and how Matthew felt she had betrayed him when she didn't do that.

"Thanks for letting me stay here, mom. You don't know how much you're helping me out."

Ava put her arm around Charlotte. "Okay. You're learning that you have to rely upon yourself, and, if you and Matthew get back together, or if you get into a relationship with another man, you won't be in the position you're in right now - panicked and scared you're going to be on the street somehow. What would you have done if I said no to your staying here?"

Charlotte shuddered even thinking of that. What would she have done if Ava had turned her down? No job, no job skills, an infant, and a husband who wanted out. If her mother didn't open her arms and doors, would she have become homeless? Perhaps for the first time, she realized just how fragile her life had been. Just how easily she could've fallen into the abyss. Thank God she had her mother. Thank God.

"I don't know the answer to that question, mom. I don't want to even think about it. I'm just grateful you're going to give me a chance. I won't let you down. That's a promise."

"Okay. I believe you. So, we need to take a couple of rooms here and move you and Siobhan into these rooms. You can stay here until you figure everything out. But I'm expecting you to do just that – spending time figuring every-thing out. This will not be a time for you to hide out from life. I know you've had a setback, Charlotte, but you can't let it break you. You have to find your strength here. If you can learn to stand on your own two feet, nothing can tear you down in the future. You can just tell the world to come at you, give you all its got, you can take it all."

Charlotte nodded her head. "Okay, mom. I'll make good use of my time here. I won't try to hide out from life. I'll figure out what I want to be when I grow up."

Charlotte drove back to Boston to get her things. When she got home, Matthew was there. "I'm moving in with my mom," Charlotte announced to him.

"On Nantucket," Matthew said. "That's good. Listen, I have a cousin who lives there. Her name is Willow."

Willow. That name sounded familiar for some reason. "What does she do?"

"I'm not sure. She's quite strange. She's into psychics and tarot and talking to dead people and whatnot. But she's connected. You might give her a shout once you get on the island."

A psychic named Willow. Damn, that sounded familiar. "Connected, how?"

"She dabbles in art. It's a hobby for her. She's quite good, too. She works with watercolors and sculpts and things like that. So, she knows a lot of artists."

"And? What does that matter that she knows artists?"

"I don't know. I thought maybe you could look for a job with one of the artists on the island, that's all."

Charlotte felt irritated for some reason. "Thanks for the advice," she said sarcastically.

"Char, don't be like this," he said.

"Don't be like what? How am I supposed to be when my husband has announced he wants to play like a bachelor instead of caring for his wife and baby? Thanks for the advice about seeing Willow, but, news flash, I wouldn't have to get a job if you acted like an adult instead of a 2-year-old. Siobhan's more mature than you are."

Charlotte knew she was being unfair. A little voice was nagging her about her role in the breakdown of the marriage. The voice reminded her that she was the one who lied about the birth control thing. She definitely was responsible for at least 50% of the situation, probably much more.

But she didn't care. At that time, she wanted to act like the wronged party. She wanted him to feel guilty for dumping her. Maybe it was emotionally manipulative, but she didn't care. She was hurting, and Matthew was going to pay.

Matthew just shook his head. "I do love you, Char. This isn't the life I want, that's all. I'm sorry."

"Yeah, I'm sorry, too. I'm sorry I ever met you."

The car was packed up by that time with all her and Siobhan's things, at least the amount of things that would fit into her room at the inn. She packed Siobhan into the car and got in herself, and drove off.

She would be starting a new life, and she had no idea what was around the corner. All she knew was that she was about to panic.

Breathe, Charlotte, breathe.

Perhaps she would forgive Matthew for dumping her like this. Maybe not.

Probably not.

Chapter Eight

Hallie

Two weeks later

Hallie waited in the doctor's office, feeling nervous. Ava was right next to her. Hallie nervously talked about what was going on with Ava's daughter, Charlotte. She needed something to take her mind off of what would happen.

For the past couple of weeks, she could think of nothing but this doctor's appointment. She was back to not sleeping at night, and no amount of acupuncture would help that. She was still meditating and going to her yoga classes, but nothing was helping. She was obsessing. She felt like she had gone backward in her life and the stress of knowing that fed upon the stress of seeing the doctor. The last thing she wanted to do was backslide, but that's what she was doing.

Before she came to the island, she was a mental mess. She was in a toxic marriage, and her daughter Morgan didn't speak with her because she smothered Morgan. She couldn't sleep most nights, drank way too much, and was so depressed that there were mornings when she didn't want to get out of bed.

That all changed when she came to Nantucket. She got a new lease on life. She met Willow, who encouraged her to bring out her inner tigress. Willow started a series of acupuncture treatments and herbal and crystal therapy, all of which changed her life. Before she knew it, she was eating better, walking every day in the sunshine, going to regular yoga class, and feeling amazing. She divorced her husband and took the money from the divorce to become Willow's business partner. She enrolled in an online degree in integrative nutrition. She made up with her daughter. Morgan came to visit her, and she went out to visit Morgan in San Francisco several times since then.

And she was so looking forward to becoming a life coach. She was still very busy with her nutrition courses because she still wanted to get a degree in integrative nutrition. That was her long-term goal. But her short-term goal was to become a life coach. She knew she had a knack for it when she helped several of the spa's clients get their lives together, just as she had. She knew what it took to go from a depressed mess to fabulous and happy. She wanted other people to experience the happiness she was experiencing every day.

Now, this. The fear was back. The sleepless nights were back. And she realized she never really recovered at all. She just managed to claw her way to a good place, but she wasn't prepared for setbacks.

Willow assured her that she would help her with her unique therapies no matter what. That somewhat put her mind at ease, but not really. Willow was amazing with the acupuncture, the herbal and crystal therapies, and even the auditory therapies with the singing bowls. But treating a serious disease was above even Willow's pay grade.

"Ms. Gleason, the doctor will see you now," a young brunette woman with curly hair said to her.

Ava squeezed Hallie's hand as the two ladies walked into the doctor's office.

A very kindly African-American woman smiled at Hallie when she walked in the door. "Hello, my name is Dr. Michaels. And you must be Hallie."

Hallie nodded her head, not knowing what to say.

Ava spoke up. "Hello, Dr. Michaels. This is Hallie, and my name is Ava. I'm her best friend. And she asked me to be here."

Dr. Michaels shook both of their hands and then turned to Hallie. "So, you're here for a physical. Has there been any cause for concern? I like to ask that question before I begin. It helps guide me."

Hallie didn't know how to tell her that she was so freaked out because a psychic told her there was something wrong. If Dr. Michaels was a true scientist, as doctors often were, she would laugh at her.

"No. I just need a breast exam, Pap smear, bloodwork, whatever you need to do."

Dr. Michaels nodded her head. "Okay. Now, let me get your vitals and listen to your breathing." She got out a stethoscope, and Hallie breathed when asked. She took Hallie's temperature and asked her to step on the scale. Then she took several vials of blood.

"Everything sounds normal," she said. "Now, I'm going to perform a Pap smear and breast exam, so I typically would ask your friend to leave the room. Of course, it's up to you."

Ava nodded her head. "I'll give Hallie some privacy. I'll be right out in the waiting room. Love you."

Hallie took a deep breath while the doctor left the room so she could change into her gown. A few minutes later, Dr. Michaels returned and performed the breast exam and Pap smear while talking about her children. Hallie was used to that. Doctors liked to distract their patients while they did these very embarrassing examinations. It never really took her mind off the invasive procedures, but, she always credited them for trying.

"Okay. Would you like your friend to come back in? I need to talk to you about a lump I felt in your breast."

Hallie's heart plunged. A lump. A lump. Suddenly, it seemed like the doctor was at the end of a long tunnel. She just nodded her head. "Yes, ask Ava to come in. I'm going to need her here."

Dr. Michaels went out of the office and came back with Ava. Ava sat down next to Hallie and took her hand.

"Okay. I felt a lump in your right breast. It could be nothing. It often is nothing. Women sometimes get cysts in their breasts. They sometimes get fibroid tumors. Both of those conditions are not serious. They would involve outpatient surgery to remove them, but there would be no follow-up treatment if that's what the issue is. Sometimes, you can even live with them, but women like to get it taken care of because if a malignant tumor ever grew, they wouldn't be able to distinguish the cancerous tumor from their existing fibroid tumors or cysts. So, for that reason alone, I would recommend surgery if that's what it is."

Hallie nodded her head, but she knew what she had was not going to be benign. No, Willow would not be warning her if there was nothing really wrong.

"How will you know if the lump is something danger-ous?" Hallie asked.

"I'm going to send you to a pathologist. I'll refer you to Dr. Wilder. He's the best in the business."

And then, Dr. Michaels painstakingly explained the biopsy procedure, what she could expect, and how long she would have to wait for the results. Then she answered all of Hallie's questions and Ava's questions. She also gave Hallie a brochure that explained all about the biopsy procedure.

"Now, don't worry. As I said, the lump is nothing to worry about the majority of the time. Think positive thoughts, don't let this keep you awake at night. I know, I know, easier said than done."

Hallie saw the pathologist a week later, who performed a biopsy on the lump in her breast.

Two days after that, Hallie was back in Dr. Michaels' office.

There, she learned her fate.

She had breast cancer.

Chapter Nine

Hallie

Hallie and Quinn were in Dr. Michaels' office when she found out the bad news. Quinn was squeezing Hallie's hand as Dr. Michaels explained that Hallie had Stage I breast cancer. "This is the best kind to have," she said. "Nobody wants cancer, of course, but if you're going to have cancer, it's best to have it at Stage I. It's very treatable with surgery, radiation and chemotherapy. There's over a 98% survival rate at this stage. And, from the biopsy results, it looks like you're a good candidate for surgery. I can schedule this surgery for two weeks from today."

Hallie could feel her blood pressure going down. It was bad, but it could definitely have been worse. She knew a little bit about cancer, and she knew that Stage I was the best stage to be in. Still, she wasn't looking forward to having surgery and chemotherapy.

She closed her eyes and realized that Willow might have saved her life. If it weren't for Willow, she wouldn't have seen a doctor this soon. She was just blissfully going along in her life, thinking she had no more problems to worry about. Willow's warning woke her up to the reality that you can never take your foot off the gas. Just when you think you're making plans, God laughs. And God was definitely laughing at her right at that moment.

Dr. Michaels explained the surgery, what she could expect, and about the chemotherapy. "I believe your tumor is large enough that you will need chemotherapy, unfortunately. You'll be assigned an oncologist after your surgery. Your oncologist will be the one who will recommend the course of treatment post-surgery. But, I would definitely be prepared to take several cycles of chemo after your tumor is removed."

Chemo. Hallie looked over at Quinn, who was visibly shaking. Quinn's brother had died of brain cancer, which meant that she went through surgery, radiation, and chemotherapy with him. Hallie hated putting her through this again. It wasn't the same situation, not at all - James, Quinn's brother, had a deadly kind of cancer that kills almost universally. Hallie's cancer was extremely treatable. Nevertheless, cancer was cancer, and she wondered if Quinn was experiencing some PTSD from it all.

Quinn smiled, but the smile looked forced. "Hallie, sugar, I'll be right there in the chemo room with you. We all will."

Hallie shook her head. "You have a life. You don't need to revolve it around me and my chemo schedule." Ava had a lot of time off now because her inn was only half full most days, and she had Jessica helping out. She would ask Ava to accompany her and maybe Sarah, who also had downtime. But not Quinn. Quinn was a busy woman between trying to raise her headstrong 13-year-old-going-on-4o-year-old genius daughter and working full-time. She also had a budding relationship with Asher Martin, the wealthy attorney Quinn hired to finalize the adoption of Emerson, Quinn's daughter.

No. The woman had so much on her plate. She wasn't going to add anything more.

"We'll cross that bridge when we come to it, won't we?" Quinn asked.

"We will."

Hallie asked a million questions, and so did Quinn. Dr. Michaels patiently answered each and every one. Hallie really wished that Dr. Michaels would be her permanent doctor for this, but she knew she would have to see a specialist, which was too bad. She was really comfortable around Dr. Michaels. She felt that the pretty young doctor listened to her and was patient.

After Hallie's visit and after she scheduled her surgery for two weeks out, Quinn and Hallie left the doctor's office. It was 2 o'clock in the afternoon, and Hallie was anxious to talk to Ava, Sarah, and everybody. She was happy because the diagnosis was not as dire as what she had been afraid of. At the same time, she was frightened. She heard so many bad things about chemotherapy – how it made you sick, how you lost your hair, how it made you tired. Still, things definitely could've been worse.

So much worse.

Chapter Ten

Hallie

That evening, everybody met over at Quinn's house. Hallie was anxious to talk to Ava and Sarah, not just because of her news. But also because she wanted to know how things were going with Ava's daughter Charlotte. She was concerned about Charlotte and dearly hoped the young girl could get things under control.

Ava's son Jackson had been in town, but he now was back in Los Angeles. He helped Charlotte move into Ava's house, along with Deacon helping as well. Ava and the girls also helped Charlotte pack, but the big stuff was moved by Jackson and Deacon. Unfortunately, Charlotte had to put everything into a storage locker because Ava's rooms were already furnished, so the furniture Charlotte moved out of her house didn't have a place in Ava's home.

"Okay, here's the deal," Hallie said to everybody as they dug into sushi, seaweed salad and sashimi from Lola 41, a popular sushi restaurant on the island. Quinn bought the goodies before their meeting that evening. "I have good news and bad news. The bad news is, I have breast cancer. The good news is, it's Stage I and completely treatable. There's a 98% survival rate for this type of cancer at this stage."

Ava put her hand to her heart and then squeezed Hallie's hand. "I was afraid of cancer for you. But it sounds like everything will be okay, so thank God for that. Thank God. What can I do to help you?"

"Just be there for me. If you can spare any time to go to my chemo sessions with me, that would be amazing. But if you can't come, I understand. You have a life, too. And be patient because I'm probably not going to be feeling very well for the next few months. I might need some chicken soup once in a while, for my soul and otherwise."

Hallie was still staying at an extended stay hotel and had been for the past several months. Before all this happened, she was looking into buying a home, but she hadn't yet closed on anything.

Quinn shook her head. "Hallie, sugar, I told you I wanted to also be there for you at your chemo sessions, and you said no. Now you're asking Ava to be there. What's up with that? Am I just liver paté over here?" she asked teasingly.

"I knew you would say something about that, Quinn. But I can't allow you to take the time out. You have enough going on between working full time, raising your brilliant and beautiful daughter, and hanging out with that beautiful man, Asher. You don't need me around."

Quinn took a bite of sushi and then smiled. "Number one, I'm not hanging out with Asher. He's a friend, and that's it, and that's all it's going to be for now. I've got too much going on to devote much bandwidth to him or any other man. But I'll give you that Emerson's a full-time job. Who knew having a genius for a daughter would be so challenging? But I still want to do whatever I can for you."

Sarah raised her hand. "Listen, I've been thinking about asking Ava about this anyways. Why don't I move out of here and move in with Ava? She's got the room, at least until next Memorial Day. Sorry, Ava, I know I'm putting you on the spot, and you can certainly say no. But I thought Hallie could move in here, so Quinn can look after her."

Quinn slapped her knee. "Sarah, that's a genius idea. Ava, what do you say? Do you want to play musical roommates with us?"

Ava laughed. "Why not? The more, the merrier, and Sarah's right – I have all kinds of room in my house now. Well, not all kinds, but I have at least one more room available for Sarah to live in. Sarah, why don't you go ahead and get moved in, and Hallie can move in here with Quinn? I'd feel better, Quinn, if I knew you were looking after Hallie. You'll do a great job with that, I know."

Hallie started to cry. "You ladies, I just don't know what I would do without any of you. You all have saved my life so many times. I just can't even express my gratitude to all of you."

All four of the ladies put their hands together in a circle. "We are all in this together."

Hallie nodded her head. She knew that that was right. "Well, my surgery is in a couple of weeks. Ava, how are things going with you? I mean, with Charlotte?"

Ava shook her head. "I wish I could say something amazing, but I can't. My daughter got herself into a real pickle, and that's putting it mildly. I always told her she needed to have an independent life because you cannot rely on a man to always be there for you. But she didn't listen to me. And now, she doesn't have options. She has to live with me, and if things don't get better between her and Matthew, and they end up divorcing, I don't know what she's going to do. We worked it out the other evening. Matthew will only be paying her about $300 a week in child support, assuming he gets another job making what he was making at the restaurant where he was working. Which was around $60,000. She can't live on $300 a week, not with Siobhan. She's going to have to find a job. But that's complicated because she has Siobhan at home."

"That's always a vicious circle, isn't it?" Sarah asked. "A single mother has to work if she wants to stay off welfare because child support is not enough to survive. But the cost of childcare is so high that it's almost impossible to work and make everything make sense. I don't know how women do it these days after their husbands leave them high and dry. How do single mothers make it all work out?"

"That's the million-dollar question, isn't it?" Ava asked. "You'd think this country would have a kind of a solution about it by now. You know, I caught the movie *9-to-5* the other night. You guys remember that movie, don't you? Dolly Parton, Lily Tomlin, Jane Fonda and a very toxic boss played by Dabney Coleman?"

Quinn started to laugh. "Oh, that movie was a hoot! I loved it! Who hasn't had fantasies about killing the boss in very creative ways?"

"Right," Ava said. "'I thought it was Skinny and Sweet!' Anyhow, it struck me that that movie was not just ahead of its time but apparently was just a fantasy after all. The ladies in that movie put things in the office like on-site daycare, and they put in changes like letting the employees job share and have flex time. And after I watched that movie, I wondered why corporate America doesn't do things like that now? If big offices had things like daycare in their buildings, and if they let women work flexibly, maybe working mothers would have a lot less stress in their lives."

"Another reason why women need to rule the world," Sarah said. "Women are just much more practical about finding solutions to problems. You're right – every big corporation, every large firm should have a daycare on-site at the very minimum. But, how would that help Charlotte?"

"Good question," Ava said. "That's another bone of contention. She has a bachelor's degree in art history. Granted, it's from a very prestigious school, Cornell. But a bachelor's degree in art history will not get her anywhere. She needed to get a Master's degree, preferably a Ph.D., and then she would be able to make her degree pay off. But, as it is, I don't know what she's even qualified to do." Ava shook her head. "I tried to guide her. I tried to tell her that she needed to either get a degree that would be useful in the world or, if she persisted in getting a degree in art history, she needed to go on with schooling. She didn't listen to me, and now here she is. No job, no good prospects, a brand-new baby, and a husband who wants out."

Hallie knew Charlotte might be a good first client for her new career. "Maybe I could brainstorm with her," Hallie said. "I can see where her interests are, what she's good at. I could set some goals for her and maybe help her look for a job that would be perfect for her. It would be great practice for my life coaching. And it would be amazing to take my mind off my own issues."

"That's a great idea," Ava said. "By the way, I'm so proud of you for branching out into the life coaching thing. So many people need that kind of thing. Not just women, but everybody. You're right. Charlotte would be a great first client for you. I'll pay you your going rate, of course."

"No. I want to do that as a favor," Hallie said.

Ava rolled her eyes. "Don't argue with me. I know life coaches make at least $75 an hour, so I'll pay you $100 per hour. No arguing," Ava said firmly.

Hallie wanted to keep arguing with her, but Ava's face told her she meant business. So, Hallie just shut her mouth. "Well, thank you. I mean, I feel uncomfortable-"

Ava put her hands together like she was going to strangle Hallie. "Just let me pay you properly. Now, Sarah, what's going on with that penny?"

Sarah shrugged her shoulders. "I looked it up on the internet, and the penny is quite valuable if it's real. But I don't think it's real, though. I'm going to Temecula tomorrow, and then I guess I'll go down to a place I found on the internet called San Diego Coin Buyers and see what they say about it. I'm not expecting much, though."

Everybody laughed. Hallie was feeling very relaxed by the end of the evening. In Charlotte, she had her first client, and she was scheduled for surgery in a couple of weeks. She knew in her heart that everything was going to be okay.

And it would be. As long as she had her girls by her side.

Chapter Eleven

Sarah

October

Sarah touched down that bright and crisp October morning at the San Diego airport. She got her bags and called an Uber to take her to the car rental place. She was used to this kind of routine, as Ava had sent her to California many times over the past year or so to meet with winery owners.

Temecula, California, was a small town about an hour north of San Diego known for its wineries. It was nestled at the foot of the Temescal Mountains, a small mountain range. The Santa Ana Mountains were close by as well.

Sarah had been to Temecula a few times, and she enjoyed going to their wineries. She had established a relationship with one winery in particular, the Europa Village Winery and Resort. The hotel was Spanish-style and sprawling, with arches, stucco, and a Spanish tile roof. Their

Bolero label was diverse, and they offered many different varietals of wine, from Moscatos, Proseccos, Chardonnays and everything in between. Sarah was particularly fond of their Garnacha varietal, a deep red wine with notes of cherry cola and baking spices, commonly found in Spain. Their Albariño was excellent, too. This traditional Mediterranean varietal was a white wine with notes of sea salt, lemon, and yellow baked Apple. There was also a hint of Asian spice in the wine, very subtle but gave the wine its punch.

Sarah enjoyed working with Raul, the owner and general manager of the winery. He always gave her a tour when she visited and encouraged her to try all their new varietals. She always got excited when there was something new to try. Usually, she would stay the night in one of the luxury bedrooms in the sprawling Spanish-style estate. But, on this day, she was anxious to get to the coin-collecting place.

She had to admit she was intensely curious about the penny and its meaning. At first, she thought nothing of it. It was odd, of course, that a penny would come in the mail like that. And, of course, it was weird because she didn't know who it came from.

After she told the girls about the penny, she did a little bit of research on it. And she found out there was a possibility that it was quite valuable. Nonetheless, she was afraid to even go there in her brain. She still wanted to see a coin collector to get a second opinion on the issue. And then she would go from there.

Now, she was really excited about the prospect that maybe it was something good for her. Because something had to happen for her. She was making okay money working for Ava, not great money. On the days she took over the running of Ava's 'Sconset Inn, she could reap the profits from it, which were substantial during the busy season.

But, now that the busy season was over, there was less for Sarah to do at Ava's inn. When the island was overrun with tourists, and Ava couldn't keep up with the guests during the summer months, Sarah was just as busy as Ava. She not only supplied the wine for the place, but she entertained the guests by recommending the best wines for their meals. She worked with the cooks and the chefs by getting wine for their dishes. She and Ava held a wine tasting every week, which was a big hit with the tourists. And there was always something to do, as far as chipping in to help Ava run the place. Even with Jessica there, Sarah was busy helping out. Jessica came to stay at the inn in July, and she took a lot of duties off of Sarah and Ava's shoulders, but they still had plenty going on.

Sarah was still busy procuring wines for Ava's place, and Ava really tried to keep her busy. But Sarah knew Ava didn't really need her that much anymore, and she probably wouldn't need her again until next summer. Ava didn't know how to tell her as much, but she knew she really should just be working part-time for Ava and earning a part-time salary as well.

Sarah thought about her plight and felt slightly stressed about it. She wasn't settled quite yet. She had been living at Quinn's house for the past few months, and now she would be staying with Ava again. In other words, she was relying on the kindness of her sister and her friends, and she really wanted to be independent. She wanted to have a place of her own, but that seemed impossible at the moment. She knew the houses on Nantucket started at $1.5 million and went up from there. You could occasionally find a home for less than that, but those homes didn't last long on the market. She didn't have enough money for a down payment for a home, and she didn't see hope that she would ever get the money for a down payment.

She increasingly thought she would have to move from the island. Anywhere else in the country, with the possible exception of San Francisco and New York, would have a lower cost of living than on Nantucket. Actually, with the median house price almost $3 million on Nantucket, even San Francisco and New York would be cheaper.

She didn't want to leave the island. She loved it. She loved the crowds of the busy season, but she also loved the solitude of the off-season. Most importantly, she had good friends and her sister on the island. If she had to move, she would be alone again.

She knew what it was like to be surrounded by people she couldn't trust. That was her life in Monterey. She had superficial women she hung out with, but none of them would go to the mattresses for her. They proved that when she was arrested for something she didn't do, and nobody would come to her aid. Now, she had ladies who had her back. That was priceless. So she did not want to have to leave the island to live anyplace else.

Sarah negotiated a contract for some more wines at the Europa Village Winery. She then headed back to San Diego to go to the coin place she found online. San Diego Coin and Bullion was located in a strip mall in the heart of San Diego's neighborhood called Hillcrest. She nervously went inside and saw a short, thin guy, probably around 25 years old. He was looking at a coin with a magnifying glass while a middle-aged lady patiently waited.

He shook his head at the lady. "I can give you five bucks for this," he said.

"Five dollars? This is a coin from the 1700s."

"Yeah, but it's in really bad shape. You can barely tell the date on the coin and not much else. I would grade this coin somewhere between poor and fair. Sorry."

The lady looked disappointed. "Well, what did I expect? I only paid $10 for it. I guess I thought I was getting a steal, but it turned out they were stealing from me."

Then the lady left. The guy grinned at Sarah. "Everybody buys stuff from yard sales, thinking they have a masterpiece that somehow went unnoticed by the yard sale's owner. They've been reading too many articles about people who pick up rare works of art at sales, like the Ansel Adams negatives picked up at a garage sale and worth $200 million. But the chances of that happening is less than winning the lottery. Anyhow, my name's Lucas. What can I do for you?"

Sarah nodded her head, liking this guy immediately. "I have a penny. It was sent to me in the mail by somebody. I think it's just a penny, but I thought I would get it checked out. I did research on it, and, I think it might be worth some money. Maybe a lot of money. But I wanted to get a professional's opinion while I was in town."

At that, Sarah gave the penny to Lucas. He took one look at it, and his eyes got wide.

"Where did you get this?" he asked as he looked at the coin. "I doubt this is real. Where did you get it?"

"As I said, it came in the mail to me. I don't even know who sent it to me. Somebody in France."

The guy shook his head. "Trust me, a rando in France is

not going to send this to you. It had to come from some-body you knew."

"Well, I think I know who sent it, but I thought she was just trying to insult me by sending me a penny in the mail."

"I don't think she was trying to insult you. If this is real, she was trying to make you very wealthy."

Sarah smiled. She was excited, because her research indicated that the penny was worth a lot of money, too. But she wanted to hear it out of this guy's mouth, because he was the professional.

"This penny is the Holy Grail of pennies. It's the Sistine Chapel of pennies. It's a 1943 copper penny, if it's real, which is a big if. Trust me, people have been trying to coun-terfeit these pennies for years. I've seen all kinds of shenani-gans involving these pennies. People who have taken a 1948 penny and have tried to somehow make the 8 look like a 3. People who have taken a 1943 silver penny and dipped it in copper. They never get away with it. So, for your sake, I hope it's real."

She thought so. Her research told her all about the background of the penny. Again, though, she was excited to hear it from the horse's mouth.

"Okay. Here's the deal," Lucas said. "During the Second World War, copper was needed to make ammuni-tion. So, the United States started making pennies out of steel, not copper. But in 1943, there were about 40 copper pennies produced. It was a mistake. The copper planchets were left in, and 40 coins were made in copper that year. 40. Only 13 have ever been known to exist in the world. 13. Wrap your head around that."

Sarah nodded along. This guy was confirming her research, and her heart was soaring with every word.

"Yeah, I mean. If this is real, again this is a big if, you

might have a $2 million penny on your hands. It's a Denver mint, and the last 1943 copper penny with the Denver mint in the shape this penny is in, which I would grade as about uncirculated, which means there's very little wear, sold for $1.7 million. In 2010. You put this baby at auction, and you could be writing your ticket."

"Actually, I knew everything you were telling me about the penny before I came here. I did research online. But it didn't seem real, which was the reason why I wanted to see you. I'm just afraid somebody took a steel penny and dipped it in copper or something."

And then she thought about it. It must've been Olivia who sent it to her, but why would she do that? She knew if anybody had a rare coin in their collection, it would be Nolan. He wasn't really a coin collector, per se, but he certainly had the money to purchase any coin he wanted. Maybe he had a fascination with this particular kind of coin. She didn't know. There was a lot she didn't know about her late boyfriend. And, apparently, just as much she didn't know about Nolan's ex-wife.

"I don't know," Lucas said. "What I do know is you need to find somebody to authenticate this for you. Listen, an organization called PCGS, Professional Coin Grading Service, can help you. You can submit the coin online and send it to them, but I wouldn't do that. God forbid that coin gets lost in the mail. I'd go to a show. They're going to be in Vegas in a couple of days. The Bellagio hotel. I'd book a room, have a fun time in Vegas, make sure you catch the Bellagio fountain show every hour on the hour and take your coin to them. They can authenticate it for you, and if they give it their seal of approval, I'd contact Sotheby's to auction it off for you."

Sarah couldn't believe her good fortune. And Vegas was

not a very long drive from where she was. She could drive there in six hours.

"Bellagio will be having it in a couple of days?" Sarah asked.

"Yeah, but it's for members only. Register for their organization online, and pay the dues. Then head over to the Bellagio Hotel and find out if you're an instant millionaire. I envy you. I see so few of these types of coins in this place."

Sarah smiled. "I'll tell you what. If they tell me it's real and I'm able to auction it off, I'll come back here and give you 1% of the auction price. That would be $20,000 if the coin really is worth $2 million."

He laughed. "Looks like you're not the only person hitting the jackpot today. Deal. Now, go on, get registered for the PCGS, and head out to Vegas. Vegas could be very lucky for you, indeed."

Was this happening? Was her financial luck finally turning around?

She certainly didn't want to look a gift horse in the mouth. The last thing she wanted to do was get her hopes up, take the penny over to this PCGS place, and have them tell her the coin was counterfeit. She certainly was not going to start spending the money in her head just yet. She was very cautious that way.

Must not get ahead of yourself. Go to Vegas, find out if it's real. And if it is real, then you can start daydreaming about buying your own cottage on Nantucket Island.

But only then.

Chapter Twelve

Sarah

Sarah drove to Vegas the next day. She really enjoyed Las Vegas, even if she wasn't a gambler. She liked the festive atmosphere of the place, how it never slept, how she could do anything she wanted to, no matter what time of the night or morning. She liked walking around and looking at all the kitschy attractions. The miniature Eiffel Tower, the miniature Empire State Building, and the miniature Champs d'Elysee all fascinated her. She actually enjoyed watching the Treasure Island shows, where pirates fight one another outside the Treasure Island hotel on the hour. She loved going into the Venice hotel and looking at the beautiful artwork that rivaled some of the paintings she saw in Europe.

Sarah had gone around the world, and she was fascinated by how Vegas attempted to fit the entire world into a few blocks. She could go from New York City, to Ancient Egypt, to Paris, to Italy, to the Circus, and to Ancient

Greece, all without leaving the confines of the Vegas strip. It was all so cheesy, but Sarah didn't care. Vegas was a town that didn't take itself seriously, and Sarah appreciated it for that reason.

She especially enjoyed the Bellagio Hotel. The beautiful hotel not just boasted amazing fountain shows set to all different kinds of music, but was luxurious inside. She also enjoyed going to the atrium and seeing the installations there. At the moment, they were displaying their autumn decorations, with enormous peacocks, trees and a fantasy Ferris Wheel.

She checked in, took her bags to the hotel room, and then called Ava. "I'm in Vegas," she said to her sister. "How are things there?"

"Fine. What are you doing in Vegas?"

"There's a coin show here. It's apparently an international organization that appraises coins, and they're having a show here at the Bellagio Hotel. It turns out that penny really might be worth some money. Maybe. If it's not counterfeit."

"Counterfeit? What do you mean?"

"I'll tell you later when I know more. Anyhow, I wanted to tell you where I was and what I'm doing. I'll be home in a couple of days. I got some really nice wine contracts for you, too. I think you'll love them."

"Good luck," Ava said. "Love you."

"Love you."

And then Sarah hung up the phone and went to see a show. She loved Blue Man Group and tried to catch them every time she was in town.

So, that's where she headed that evening.

Chapter Thirteen

Charlotte

Charlotte was determined that she would get her life back on track, one way or another. It was becoming apparent her mother was right all along – she was going to have to become her own white knight. Her mother warned her that she'd be left in the lurch if she became dependent upon a man and something happened to him.

And, lo and behold, something *did* happen to her husband. He became a selfish fool.

So, she was going to have to stand on her own two feet, and, as hard as it was going to be, she would have to get back out there and try to find work. Not just work, but a genuine career where she could afford childcare for Siobhan and somehow become fulfilled. Of course, the problem was the same as before – an actual career was hard to come by.

Still, she pictured herself as a single mother and shuddered. Matthew wasn't going to be in Siobhan's life much, except as an occasional weekend father and maybe a week here and there in the summertime. And, since he never wanted Siobhan in the first place, he probably wouldn't even want that much visitation with their daughter.

She pictured her life without Matthew. Trying to find daycare, dealing with Siobhan completely on her own, working and not seeing her daughter for 40+ hours a week. Just the thought of what awaited her filled her with dread and fear. Would she be around when Siobhan took her first step, said her first word, lost her first tooth, or would the daycare people be the ones who witnessed these milestones?

Yet, that was the realistic view of her future life. Unless she lived with her mother forever, free of charge, there was no other scenario that made sense to her. And she knew that she couldn't stay at the 'Sconset Inn forever. It wouldn't be fair for her to permanently take one of her mother's rooms away from her, because each room commanded top dollar during the busy season - $400 a night per room. That was $12,000 a month for just one room. No way could she deprive her mother of that income after depriving her of the $300,000+ her mother spent on her education.

So, she worked with Hallie that evening to try to find something she could do that could fulfill her, bring her a salary and somehow allow her to stay home with Siobhan.

Hallie sat down with her, going through a spreadsheet of how she could use her art degree to find a meaningful job.

It was a challenge, considering Charlotte's limitations. She didn't want to leave her daughter with a nanny or a daycare service. She needed to make enough money to support herself and Siobhan. And she did not plan on getting an advanced degree.

Hallie brainstormed with her, and they both hit on the idea of freelance writing. When she lived in New York, she'd gotten to know many local artists and attended many gallery openings and showings. She'd also attended just about every special exhibition that came to the city. Then she would write about the artists, the gallery openings and showings and the exhibitions and would submit the articles to publications around the country.

Because she was a decent writer who had a certain flair to her critiques and interviews and articles, she was fortunate enough to see many of her freelance articles published in prominent art magazines. She really enjoyed writing arts-related content, and she discovered early on that she had a real knack for it. Her writing voice was sardonic yet light, slightly snarky yet knowledgeable. She always took her pieces seriously, always brought them in on time, and she had received letters of praise from editors for her work.

"Okay, Charlotte, this is a good lead," Hallie said. "Now, the first thing we need to do is look online to see who might need a freelance writer. But I also want to get you to identify some of the mental blocks you might have. I have a feeling you might have some. One of the things I try to do is help my clients overcome anything that might be standing in their way, including themselves. So, tell me how you feel about this idea and what you see as your chances of success. And how we can work together to ensure you can be successful."

Hallie was pinpointing what was on Charlotte's mind. "I feel I can't succeed in a competitive field like freelance writing. I know I'm a good writer, but so are many other people. What makes me stand out over all the other people who would be dying to work from home writing articles? And I also feel like I can't make enough money being a freelancer to survive."

Hallie nodded her head. "Okay. I figured that was probably your mental block. So I want you to visualize a time in your life when you didn't have those same mental blocks. When you were in school, you successfully submitted articles to art publications. What was going through your mind then? Why did you feel then that you would be successful, but you don't feel the same way now?"

Charlotte had to think about that one. "I don't know. I just had more confidence in myself back then somehow. I feel like I have nothing to bring to the table now. I didn't feel like that back then. Back then, it seemed that the world was my oyster."

"And now? What changed?" Hallie asked her.

"I got out of all that intellectual stuff, and I just became a mother. My focus has been on Siobhan and Matthew ever since Siobhan's been born. And before Siobhan was born, my focus was on Matthew. It wasn't on myself. Before I met Matthew, when I was in school, my focus was on myself and my passion, which was art. I really threw myself into it. I wish I could get back to that girl. I was so much more inter-esting to myself back then."

Hallie smiled. "Trust me, I know where you're coming from. I know the feeling of losing yourself to somebody else. It's a scary thing when you feel your soul has just disap-peared and merged with someone else's soul. So, that is what you need to do. You need to find the Charlotte that was so passionate about art and life back in college. My assignment to you is to find the articles you wrote in college, read them, and picture yourself writing them. Where were you when you wrote this article? What inspired you to write the article? I want to do that for every one of the articles you wrote in college. And I want you to do the same thing for the papers you wrote for your teachers. I want you to have renewed confidence in your writing and analytical abilities. For a good reason, you've gotten away from that – when you're so busy taking care of another living being, you don't really have time to see the trees. But that's what you need to do. See the trees."

After that, Hallie went up to Charlotte's room. She helped organize everything on her desk, showing her how to file everything so she could find research at the drop of the hat. "And, maybe even more important, is the concept of Feng Shui."

Charlotte knew something about Feng Shui. At least she had heard of the concept, but she wasn't quite sure what it meant. "How will we make my bedroom more Feng Shui?"

Hallie smiled. "This is a beautiful room and set up so it's relaxing. That's very important for your mind. You know what they say – a cluttered space produces a cluttered mind. That's why your bedroom must stay minimalist. It's good you don't have a computer here. Your bedroom should be a place for you to sleep and not a place where you will feel stressed. Ava really does get the concept of Feng Shui, so she uses neutral colors in the bedroom, and the sheets are white with minimal patterns. It's good the ceiling fan is not directly above the bed, and all the natural light coming into the room is very helpful as well. You mustn't clutter this room. It should be a sanctuary for you. A place to relax."

Charlotte walked around the room. "What else makes this room Feng Shui?"

"The symmetry and the angles. The space on either side of the bed is symmetrical. The artwork is placed carefully, so it's soothing. There are no large mirrors or bulky artwork or anything that doesn't belong. Keep your bedroom that way. That'll be very important for your mental health, which will, in turn, be very important for finding a job. Finding a job is almost all mental. You need to be tough and have a thick skin. You might have to go through many rejections, but that is a good thing. Remember, even the best baseball player misses 70% of the pitches."

Charlotte smiled. "Okay, that's right. Thank you, this has been very helpful for me."

"Good. In our next session, we will go and do the research on people who might be looking for a good art writer. You never know. You just might find what you're looking for around the corner."

When Hallie left, Charlotte was feeling a bit more confident. But just a bit. She knew a lot of the rejection would be coming her way. As much as she wanted to avoid that, she knew she couldn't.

She was just going to have to learn to live with it.

Chapter Fourteen

Sarah

Sarah went to the PGCS show the next day at the Bellagio. There were individual tables set up all around the ballroom. Behind every table was a man with a lanyard talking to somebody.

She did a little research on the PGCS. She now knew it was the gold standard for coin appraisals. She just wasn't sure what the procedure was. After standing in line, she approached one of the tables and sat down.

She showed him the penny, and he nodded his head. "I'm going to have to have this authenticated. If you leave this with me, you can pick it up at the end of the show. Our appraiser's on-site and will let you know if it's real or counterfeit."

He was much more all-business than the guy in San Diego, which Sarah appreciated. At the same time, she didn't feel nearly as comfortable with this guy as she did with Lucas in San Diego.

"What do you charge?"

"If this is real, we will charge $300 up front, and then 1% of the sale price. And there's a 24 hour turnaround."

"Thank you," she said. "Where do I pick the coin up?"

He directed her to another table where individuals were picking up coins in plastic baggies. "That's where. Let me give you a ticket that you'll need to present when you pick up your coin. Good luck with this. This could be one helluva find if it's real."

Sarah felt her heart pounding. She was having a great time in Vegas, going to the casinos and playing the slots here and there, seeing the Blue Man group, just walking around and seeing the sights. But that wasn't the reason why she was there. She was there to see if there was a possibility she was an instant millionaire. She needed to find out if she would be going to a Sotheby's auction where it was possible she'd come away with $2 million or more.

Again, she didn't want to get her hopes up. There was always a possibility that some clever person took a 1948 copper penny and chiseled off a part of the number eight so it looked like a three. She looked on the internet after she talked to Lucas and found out that was what people did. She had no way of knowing if that was what had happened. Apparently, the people here would know this. And that's what she was looking forward to.

The next day, Sarah paid her fee and picked up her coin at the end of the show. It was accompanied by an authentication certificate, complete with the PGCS seal of approval.

Sarah's heart started to pound.

She would have to find an auction house.

Chapter Fifteen

Hallie

It was a day of Hallie's surgery, and she was extremely nervous. She knew what to expect, as she had met with the surgeon who would be working on her. It seemed a pretty straightforward procedure. And she wasn't worried because she knew the surgeon, Dr. Wallace, was very skilled and experienced.

She knew she would experience a lot of pain after the surgery. Willow was ready to perform some of her magic on her, as she was very skilled with the acupuncture and she also said to Hallie that she had a few other tricks up her sleeve that would help with the pain. What those tricks were, Hallie didn't know. But she knew Willow was a very skilled healer, and Willow would help her with her recovery.

On the day of the surgery, Ava was with her. "How long does the surgery take?" Ava asked.

"About an hour." Truth be told, Hallie was nervous because there was always a possibility that the cancer had spread. Her other doctor told her she was in stage one, but perhaps the cancer had spread since then. The doctor was going to check her lymph nodes, just to be on the safe side. She wouldn't know the results of those tests for another few days. Another few days of pins and needles.

Her name was called, and she went into a room and had her vitals checked, changed into her gown, and the surgeon came to see her to see how she was doing. She was taken to the anesthesiologist, and she counted back from 100. She counted 98, and then started to float euphorically.

The next thing she knew, she was in the recovery room. She was freezing, so she took the thin blanket that was on her, and pulled it up to her chin. She was extremely groggy, and Ava came back to see her.

"You did well," she said. "How do you feel?"

Hallie felt the bandages on her breast. So far, there wasn't pain, but that was because she was still feeling the effects of the anesthesia. "I guess I feel okay. Surgery is so disorienting. One second you're counting back from 100, and the next you're waking up."

Ava laughed. "I know what you mean. It does seem like that, doesn't it?"

"When can I go home?" Hallie asked.

"I'll go check." Ava left and came back. "If you're feeling up to it, you can leave right now."

Ava helped Hallie get into her clothes, and a nurse came around with a wheelchair. Hallie climbed into the wheelchair, and the nurse wheeled her to Ava's car.

Ava drove Hallie to Quinn's home, where she was staying for the time being. Quinn was there, as she had taken off work that day. She and Ava helped Hallie to her bedroom, where Hallie rested her head and fell right to sleep.

The next few weeks were a time for Hallie to recover before starting her chemo treatments. Since Quinn could not be around all the time, and Hallie needed nursing care, Hallie had a lady name Maria come in and help her with changing her bandages, giving her sponge baths, and making sure she took her pills. While Quinn was home, however, she did all that, too.

Hallie was also amazed that Quinn's little daughter, Emerson, was also a big help. "Hey," Emerson said to Hallie. "I've got this. My mom, she was sick for a while, and I did all I could for her. She was having issues with her heart, she had heart failure, so she couldn't get around very much. I don't know what I can do to help, but I can certainly play music for you. I've always been told music therapy is the best kind of therapy there is."

Emerson played for Hallie as much as Hallie wanted, which was quite a bit. Hallie always loved the violin. She always loved any kind of string instrument, such as a cello, the viola, the bass and the violin. She was groggy much of the time because of her pain killers, but she still wanted to hear Emerson play. The young girl was such an amazing musician. Her playing was nuanced and diverse. She could break Hallie's heart with a piece, and then go right into an up-tempo song that made Hallie want to dance and sing.

Some evenings, when Hallie was feeling a bit better, she and Quinn and Emerson would play a board game, or watch a movie together. Sometimes they were joined by Joe, Emerson's boyfriend. Joe was a pale redheaded kid who really seemed to adore Emerson, and he seemed like such a good young man. Emerson and Joe had an easy rapport -

teasing each other, laughing at each other's jokes, just basically getting each other.

About a month after her surgery, it was time to get serious. She soon would be starting her chemotherapy. She was feeling a lot better, and she recovered from the pain of the surgery.

But now, things would get real.

And she was very nervous about that.

Chapter Sixteen

Hallie

Before starting chemo, Hallie sat down with her oncologist. His name was Dr. Raymond, and he explained everything about the next process. He told her all about chemotherapy, what to expect, where to get it, and what the side effects would be.

Sarah was with her for this visit. Her friend had been bouncing off the walls lately because she apparently possessed a very valuable penny. She'd already contacted an auction house. Because her coin was authenticated by the gold standard of coin authentication, Sotheby's had agreed to put the coin in its next auction. It was all very exciting. So, she and Sarah had something to talk about in the waiting room before seeing the oncologist. Something that did not involve cancer cells, and Hallie was so grateful for that.

After Dr. Raymond told her what to expect with chemo, he handed her a folder, and Hallie opened it up and looked at it a little bit. She flipped through it. She saw that Dr. Raymond advocated for certain kinds of alternative therapies to go along with the usual radiation, chemotherapy, and surgery. Specifically, he advocated for the use of acupuncture and marijuana.

Acupuncture she knew about, of course, and was a firm believer in it. But cannabis was something else. Would she go that route?

"I understand the chemo will make me nauseated, and you will prescribe anti-nausea drugs."

"Yes. Zofran is the drug I typically prescribe for that."

Hallie nodded her head. "I've taken that before. It seems to work well." She hesitated, but she was interested in another doctor's recommendation for her treatment protocol. "I also see you advocate for medical marijuana," she tentatively said. "Tell me more about that."

"Well, as you know, in Massachusetts, cannabis is fully legal for anybody over the age of 21. When treating cancer patients, I always prefer to give information about cannabis so the patients can make up their minds about it."

Hallie shifted uncomfortably in her chair. "What does it do? How does it help?"

"It helps with increasing appetite, decreasing nausea and minimizing pain. Zofran is excellent for decreasing nausea, and I could prescribe Oxycodone for pain, but cannabis really helps because it makes you desire food. It's very important that you eat properly during your treatment and do not lose too much weight, and cannabis would help with that."

Hallie felt incredibly square when Dr. Raymond told her about how he wanted her to start smoking pot. She had never tried it. Even in college, when almost everybody she knew was passing around the bong, she never tried it when they offered it to her. She had graduated from college in 1989 from the University of Missouri. During that period of time, marijuana wasn't legal anywhere. So, she knew the kids smoking it when she was in college were getting it illegally. She was always afraid it would somehow be laced with something that could harm her. She was also terrified of getting busted and tossed out of school.

Of course, times had changed. And, oh, how they had changed! More and more states were legalizing pot. Yet, she was still apprehensive about it. She believed pot made you lazy, and she had spoken to too many high people. She would ask them a question, and they would answer her approximately 10 minutes later. That is, if they even remembered she asked them a question.

Hallie decided to find out some information about what the doctor had told her. So, she got on her phone, found a medical marijuana dispensary online and decided to check it out.

After she and Sarah got out of the doctor's office, Hallie suggested they go there. "What do you think, Sarah? You want to check out the dispensary here on the island with me?"

Sarah grinned. "Why not? Listen, I'm all for anything that will help you recover. And if medical marijuana increases your appetite and decreases your nausea, I say we go for it."

Outside the shop, called the Green Lady Dispensary, was a guard who informed her that she had to show her ID, which she did, and she was allowed to go into the gleaming room. It was a very elegant and modern space, with overhead lighting and glass cases filled with paraphernalia and small bins with the green dried weed in them. She smiled as she looked at all the different yummy-looking treats in another glass case. There were cookies, rice crispy treats, and lollipops of every color. There were chocolate bars, gummy bears and brightly colored drinks. Behind every gleaming glass case was a young person who looked like they were only too happy to help.

The way the glass cases were arranged, with the overhead lighting and the salespeople behind every case, made the place look like the makeup counter at Macy's. Of course, instead of perfumes and eyeshadows, there were little green buds that had names such as Bubba Kush, Jillybean, Purple Urkle, Blue Dream, Willy's Wonder and Fruity Pebbles.

At first, she tried not to make eye contact with the young salespeople because she didn't want to buy anything. But her curiosity had become insatiable, as she really wanted to ask a few questions.

So, she approached a tall and gangly guy who gave her a friendly smile. "Are you a new client?" he asked.

"Uh, I don't know."

"Oh. I was just going to say that if you're a new client, we're offering either 10% off your purchase or a free edible."

"Edible? I'm sorry, I don't know what you mean."

At that, the gangly guy swept his hand over the case that had brownies, cookies, cupcakes, and candy. "You can choose from anything in this case."

Hallie leaned down and took a closer look at the goodies. They looked normal, like something that she might buy at any bakery. In fact, they looked extremely tempting. "I don't know." She started to wring her hands. "I just wanted to get some information. You see, my doctor told me to come here. I mean, not come here exactly, but he told me that marijuana might be a good thing for me."

Gangly guy nodded solemnly. "I see. You have a medical issue, and your doctor recommended marijuana for it. If that's the case, I recommend you get your medical marijuana card. If you have a medical issue, you'll save money. Here in Massachusetts, if you have your medical marijuana card, you don't have to pay taxes on your purchase. If you don't have a card, you must pay a 20% sales tax plus local tax. That can add up."

Hallie nodded her head. "I guess that's what I'll do. Get a doctor's excuse for this cannabis. I need to talk to my oncologist about that. Anyhow, tell me a little bit about edibles versus non-edibles and what you offer."

So, for the next half hour, the guy explained all about different kinds of cannabis. They were apparently two main kinds of marijuana —Sativa and Indica. The Indica was the stuff that relaxed you, the Sativa was the stuff that pepped you up a bit. And then there were the hybrids, a combination of the Sativa and the Indica. Also, there were different grades of the weed. The guy, whose name was Cameron, explained patiently about everything Hallie needed to know about the different grades. He seemed very knowledgeable, so Hallie walked away from the place feeling like she had the information she needed.

She wasn't quite sure that cannabis was the way to go. But that was an option, so that was important to her.

Chapter Seventeen

Sarah

After Sarah went with Hallie to her first appointment with the oncologist, she went home and stared at her penny. It was amazing, really. It looked like a penny. It felt like a penny. But it was a penny unlike any other, except for maybe 11 others in the entire world.

She had already submitted her penny online at Sotheby's, and they had accepted her coin for their next auction. It was definitely exciting, but it all seemed so surreal.

As she looked at the penny, she wondered again how it came to her.

So, she decided that she was going to do one thing. If this whole thing came to fruition, she would make a point to find Olivia and try to find out why she would send this to her. Because, in Sarah's mind, there was no doubt Olivia was behind all this. No doubt in her mind at all.

But why?

Chapter Eighteen

Hallie

Hallie went to her first chemo appointment. She sat in the comfortable chair, hooked up to a drip that put the poisonous chemicals into her veins. Ava was sitting next to her, chatting about everything under the sun. Everything, except for what was going on with her.

"And Charlotte, I just don't know want to do with that girl," Ava said. "You really helped her because she needs to focus on her future. But it's been hard to keep her on track. She's been kind of up and down. Sometimes she mopes around, wanting to get back with Matthew. Other times, she really gets motivated to find a job. And then she falls back on moping about Matthew again."

That sounded familiar to Hallie. "Here's the thing. It's never just a straight line. She's grieving, in her way. She thought her life would be one way, and it's not. And she doesn't really know what to do. I'm going to continue to work with her because I need to. I need to focus on something other than my cancer. So, as soon as I feel better, I will help her."

Ava smiled. The two of them were eating popsicles. Hallie's popsicle was blue and flavored with raspberry. Ava's popsicle was red and cherry-flavored. The popsicles apparently helped chemo patients because they prevented mouth sores. Hallie was learning so much. Unfortunately, the things she was learning were things she hoped she never would have to learn. She never thought she'd be in a position to be sitting and taking chemotherapy next to her best friend in the whole world. Yet, there they were.

She also did her research on the whole cannabis issue. It apparently was extremely helpful for chemotherapy patients, so she knew she would probably use that when she got home.

Hallie tried to relax. There was a movie showing, and if Ava were not there, she would probably be focused on that. It was a romantic comedy starring Sandra Bullock. She wasn't sure which one it was since Sandra Bullock was the queen of the romantic comedy for a while, but it looked good.

"I hope you can help Charlotte," Ava said. "You know, it's funny. I always assumed it would be Samantha who was going to need my handholding throughout her life. But she's squared away. She's doing great. And my daughter Charlotte, the one who graduated from Cornell, the one who married fairly well, she's the one who's the mess. But I can't complain."

Hallie closed her eyes. She was starting to feel sleepy. She knew that was perfectly normal, as one of the drugs going into her veins had a sedative effect. "Keep talking," she said to Ava. "It's important I still hear your voice."

But then she drifted off to sleep.

Ava drove her home, and Quinn was already there.

She got home after the chemo session and immediately retched. She took her Zofran, but that didn't seem to help. She lay in bed, doubled over in pain, and nausea seemed to hit her out of nowhere. Then, without warning, she was vomiting into the trash can by her bed.

She felt so weak that she couldn't get out of bed to make it to her adjoining bathroom. She pulled the covers over her head and took several deep breaths before dragging herself over to the bathroom and lying next to the toilet. It wasn't long before she was emptying out the contents of her stomach again. She felt grateful to be next to the bathroom whenever this extreme nausea hit.

Quinn's dog, Kona, a beautiful rescue mutt, was right there in the bathroom next to her. Kona lay down on the cold tile and just stared at Hallie, and then nudged Hallie with her cold, wet nose. Hallie weakly put her arm around the dog and stood up and washed her face.

"Quinn," Hallie said. "I think I'll need more of this Zofran. And, as much as I don't want to take opiates, I'm in so much pain I'll need my Oxycontin. Could you please go and pick them up for me?"

"Sure," Quinn said. "I'll go to the pharmacy and pick them up. Will you be okay while I'm gone?"

"Yes. Just please help me back to my bed. I need to get some sleep, even though I don't know how I can when I feel like this. But I need to get into bed and pull the covers over my head and try to rest. I have the trash can by my bed, so I apologize if you have to clean up when you get back."

"That's what I'm here for," Quinn said with a smile. "I'll see you in about an hour."

"Thanks."

Ava was there, too, and she helped Hallie into bed.

Hallie groaned as she pulled the covers completely over her head. Kona jumped up and lay next to her, and Hallie held the dog close to her.

And then she willed herself to die. She felt so horrible that death would be preferable to how she was feeling at that moment.

"Ava, can you do me a favor?" Hallie asked her best friend.

"Anything, what do you need?" Ava asked.

"I found a cannabis chef online. His name is Sebastian Michel. Can you call him and schedule him to show me how to make cannabis food?"

"Sure," Ava said.

Sebastian Michel had an Instagram page that featured the cannabis dishes he made for private parties, along with delectable pastries that were cannabis-infused.

Hallie had researched this Sebastian Michel and found he had been a chef at a Michelin-starred restaurant in Boston and had even been on Gordon Ramsay's *Master Chef* show one season, where he placed fourth. She had to admit that the food and pastries he featured on his Instagram page looked beyond divine - he apparently could infuse cannabis into any food because it was all a matter of using cannabis-infused oil and butter when making his dishes.

Ava came back into the room. "We're in luck. Sebastian had a cancellation. He'll be making dinner at 7 tonight."

Hallie called Quinn.

"Uh, Quinn, I scheduled something for tonight. I probably should've checked with you first, and I'm sorry I didn't. But a guy is coming over this evening to make dinner for me. He's uh, a cannabis chef."

Quinn started to laugh. "Oh, I'm so sorry, Hallie. I

didn't mean to get a chuckle out of this. It's just that I've never heard of such a thing. You mean there's a guy who comes to people's houses and makes things like magic brownies and things like that?"

"By the pictures, I'd say that he can do much better than just making brownies," Hallie said. "Much better."

"Well, that sounds like fun," Quinn said. "Although you know I don't get into it myself. I'm sure he can make something non-cannabis too, right?"

"He can," Hallie said. "So, you're okay with having a little dinner party here tonight?"

"Count me in," Quinn said. "What about Ava and Sarah? Do you think they'll want to be there, too?"

"Sure, uh, wait," Hallie said. "Actually, Ava, could you call Sebastian back? We can't have it here, not with Emerson running around. Why didn't I think of that?"

"Oh, I thought of that," Ava said. "I'm sorry, I should've been more clear. The party will be at my place. On the terrace. I'll reserve the terrace right now so that guests can't go up there tonight."

Then Quinn started to laugh again. "We'll be having it all with a glass of wine. I guess that's irony for you. I don't get into smoking pot or eating it, for that matter, but I do love other mind-altering substances. Couldn't live without my bottle of Pinot Gris."

"I was the same way," Hallie said. "I'm still too embarrassed to go back to the dispensary, so I'm calling Sebastian to come in and make me things. I don't know. I guess I'm still the 18-year-old Freshman in college who's terrified of getting booted out of school for taking a hit off of a bong. Not that MU would've booted me out for that, because God knows everybody was doing it back then, but I was always terrified of that."

"Yet I'm sure you drank your share of wine coolers in your dorm," Quinn teased.

"Are you kidding me? I think Bartles and Jaymes sponsored my freshman year," Hallie said with a smile. "Also illegal at the age of 18. Such a mess of contradictions."

"Well, we all are," Quinn said. "At any rate, I'll see you when I get home, and I'll call Ava for you to see if she wants to partake in the festivities. It'll be fun."

Hallie smiled as she realized the pills were working. She was less nauseous and had less pain, but she still wasn't hungry. Hopefully, the cannabis could remedy that because she knew she couldn't afford to lose weight.

Then Hallie got an idea. She would invite Willow.

She texted her, and Willow immediately texted back.

"Sounds good. See you then."

And then, to Hallie's surprise, Emerson came into the bedroom. "Dude, I thought I overheard Ava talking to a cannabis chef. What's going on?"

Emerson was only 13 years old, but she was an old soul in many ways. It wasn't just that she was so darned intelligent. She was also worldly. She seemed to know things that she shouldn't know at her age. So Hallie felt she could talk to Emerson more or less as an adult.

"Yeah, there will be a guy making food for my friends and me if they want to partake. And it's going to be cannabis-infused."

"Rad. I know all about that kind of thing. I mean, I don't smoke pot myself. I know people who do, though. Of course. I think it's great you're going to be trying that. Quinn told me you were going through a tough time with your chemo. Or you would be. If there's anything I can do, I'll be happy to help."

Hallie smiled. "Are you to be okay hanging out here tonight?"

"Actually, I'm gonna be hanging out at my friend's house. Parker. She lives down the street. Quinn doesn't always like me going to a friend's house during the week, but she told me I could tonight. So, if you guys want to have your party here, you can. Trust me, I won't try to sneak any leftover brownies."

Hallie laughed. "I'm really anxious to try one of the brownies, to be honest with you."

She was actually looking forward to that evening, to her surprise.

Chapter Nineteen

Hallie

Around 7 that evening, everybody was ready to meet Sebastian.

"Dude," Willow said. "I have to admit, I was beyond intrigued by your invite to this. I've always wanted to attend one of these parties, but I've never gotten the chance. So, thanks for asking me."

"I'm glad you could come," Hallie said.

The doorbell rang, and Quinn eagerly went to answer it. On the other side was Sebastian.

Sebastian Michel was a breathtakingly handsome man who looked around 50 years old. He had twinkling blue eyes, dark curly hair and dimples when he smiled. He was long and lean and had a ready grin. Hallie took one look at him and knew she didn't just want to take cannabis classes from him. Then she felt embarrassed to even be thinking that way.

"Hey," Sebastian said when he came through the door.

He had a couple of large insulated bags - one that apparently had the food in it, and the other had his tools of the trade. "I hope you guys are all ready for a culinary experience unlike anything you've ever encountered. Now, who is the hostess for this party?"

Hallie raised her hand.

Sebastian smiled and handed her a brownie. "Don't eat this just yet. Save it for later. Although I will readily admit that I call this my 'better than sex' brownie. You'll see what I mean when you bite into it."

Hallie took the brownie and smelled it. The scent of rich chocolate and coffee filled her nose, and she immediately found that she was hungry. She hadn't been hungry that entire day, but the smell of this brownie stimulated her senses enough to make her mouth water with anticipation.

"Thank you," Hallie said to him. "This is my first time doing something like this. In fact, this is my first time smoking pot. Well, not necessarily smoking, but you know what I mean. So, I'll admit I'm very nervous."

Sebastian smiled and put his arm around her. "Don't be nervous. In fact, I will hazard a guess to say that all your nerves will be gone by the end of the evening. That's the whole point of a party like this. Just to relax around like-minded friends. Now, of course, we all have the option to either have food cannabis-infused or not. So, whoever wants their food straight, let me know."

"I really would like just regular food, if you don't mind," Ava said. "I tried marijuana in college, and I hated it. It made me paranoid, spaced out, and just out of it. I only did it once, and that was enough."

Quinn nodded her head. "Me too."

"Well, that's not a problem, of course," Sebastian said. "But I hope I don't insult you when I say you were doing it wrong if you felt spaced-out and paranoid after you smoked. Probably you were getting the wrong strain, the wrong amount, or, if you were in college, it might've been ditch weed. Most college kids get that kind of weed because it's sometimes hard to find anything else, and it's relatively cheap."

Ava cocked her head. "Ditch weed? What do you mean by that?"

"It's the kind of weed you might find growing in a ditch. And ditch weed is not the same as high-grade cannabis, I can tell you that. At any rate, you can try some of the pasta I'm making, or you can beg off. I'm flexible and not offended either way. To each your own."

"Where is Charlotte, by the way?" Hallie asked.

"She took Siobhan to see my mother," Ava said. "She'll be upset she missed this, that's for sure. She loves to try new experiences."

Everybody followed Sebastian into the kitchen. Hallie stood next to him as she watched him put some bud into the oven. "This is the first thing I have to do. It's called decarbing the bud. I have to have it in the oven for around 30 minutes, turning it over every 10 minutes. Now, this is going to be like a cooking show, because, while I'm showing you what I need to do to make the cannabutter, I'm not going to actually make all of you wait around 30 minutes while this cooks in the oven. I have my own decarbed cannabis. All of you can see what I do to make the cannabutter and cannabis-infused oil, which will be the basis for most of the foods that I'm going to make tonight."

Sebastian added the decarbed bud to some melted butter and then strained the butter with the cheesecloth. "Okay, now for the fun stuff. We're going to make cannabis pasta with clams, green chilis, shallots, shishito peppers, a cubanelle pepper, garlic, capers, white wine, crème fraîche, lime juice, and caviar."

Everybody watched him as he blended the olive oil with the mint, parsley, and chives, then took out a cast-iron skillet and heated the oil. He added the poblano, the cubanelle, and the shishito peppers into the pan, cooked it for about three minutes, and added some shallot, garlic, and capers. He let it cool for a little while, then stirred in the cannabis butter. Then, he simmered some sliced shallots, and crushed garlic with some wine and brought it to a boil in another pot. Then he added the clams, covered up the pot and steamed them. Next, he discarded the clams' shells after the clams opened and strained the liquid through a sieve into a bowl. While all this was going on, he was boiling some pasta.

Next, he took out another pot, got some regular butter, and added the clams, the crème fraîche, and some clam cooking liquid. It combined well, and he cooked it for about three minutes, and then he stirred some more cannabis butter, some lime juice, and some more mint.

Then he did the same thing without the cannabis butter. "For Ava and Quinn," he said with a wicked grin. "Oh, you're missing out. But I understand."

Ava and Quinn looked at each other. "Oh, what the hell," Quinn said. "I'm not speaking for Ava, but you only live once, and I'm all about trying new experiences. I'll try the pot pasta."

Ava grinned. "Me too. YOLO, right?"

Hallie smiled. "YOLO."

"Ava and Quinn, join the fun!" Sebastian said with a huge smile.

Hallie was watching Sebastian, trying to learn. "So, if I

can learn to make this cannabis butter or cannabis-infused oil, I can make just about anything."

"That's right. You can certainly make most things with cannabis butter or oil. Of course, the secret is to know how much to put in, what the ratios are, and how to treat the cannabis before you put it into the oil. I think you all will be pleasantly surprised when you try the pasta. It's very subtle, but it's potent in its own right."

He brought a salad to the table, along with the pasta. The salad was made with baby greens, beets, walnuts, maple syrup, balsamic, olive oil, and goat cheese. Stuffed mushrooms with goat cheese and crab were also presented. He had also brought some fresh-baked bread and gave everybody the option of putting cannabis butter on it if they wanted to get a little extra high, or just put regular herbal butter on the bread.

Hallie nervously took a bite of the pasta and then rolled her eyes in ecstasy. The pasta was divine. It was smooth and buttery and cheesy, with just enough heat, but not too much. She could not taste the cannabis at all.

"When are we going to start to feel this?" Hallie asked Sebastian.

"It depends on your metabolism, but probably within the hour."

Hallie looked around the room and saw everybody enjoyed the meal as much as she did because there was plenty of oohing and aahing. The salad and the stuffed mushrooms were also divine.

"Sugar, this meal is the best I've ever had," Quinn said enthusiastically to Sebastian. She sipped her wine and raised her eyebrows.

"I agree," Ava said. "Oh my God, I think I've died and

gone straight to heaven." She, too, took a sip of her wine and nodded her head. "Died and gone to heaven."

For her part, Willow was eagerly eating the pasta and putting a little bit of cannabis butter on her bread.

Willow raised her eyebrows and smiled. "Oh my God, it's better than sex, this food." She took a sip of her wine. "And I'm going to be feeling all of this soon, I can assure you."

As she ate her food, Hallie had to agree with her friends that this food was amazing. But she really was looking forward to how the bud made her feel. And, at first, she didn't feel anything.

But, sure enough, after about an hour, she started to feel just a little bit floaty. And, even though she wasn't all that hungry when Sebastian arrived, she was suddenly ravenous.

To her surprise, she could have conversations with everybody around the table. She felt as if she had had two glasses of wine and not more than that. She didn't feel spacey, but she definitely felt relaxed, and she felt hungrier than she had in a long, long time.

"So," Sebastian said to Hallie. "I'm curious about what brought you to me?"

"My doctor recommended I try medical cannabis. He said it would help with my appetite and my pain. And I have to admit, he was probably right. I not only am not feeling any pain right now, but I'm starving. All I can think about is that chocolate brownie you gave me, but I think it would be too much if I ate it. By the way, you are an absolutely divine cook. I mean chef."

He nodded his head and smiled. "I aim to please. And, if you would like to have more individualized instructions, I can work with you. I make house calls, but you can also come to my cooking studio. It's in The Historic District, right by the water. You seemed very keen on watching everything I was doing tonight, and I can give you instructions on adding just the right amount of weed into the butter."

Hallie knew she was going to take him up on that offer. And soon. Not just because she was anxious to learn but also because he was so damned good-looking. Then she felt embarrassed for thinking that.

She was going to have to book a session. Just as soon as she got up the nerve.

At the end of the evening, Willow put her arm around her. "Tomorrow, come to my house. I can do a ritual on you that I save for extreme situations."

Hallie nodded her head. "I'll be there."

Chapter Twenty

Hallie

The next day, Hallie told Quinn that she was going to Willow's house and not to expect her back for the entire day. Willow had explained that the healing ritual that she had planned for her was involved and would take many hours.

She'd been inside Willow's house once before, but she never actually got to see Willow's workspace. At least, she didn't have the opportunity to see Willow's healing workspace, or whatever it was that Willow called it.

She passed by the new paintings and sculptures that Willow was working on and followed the young girl behind some French doors into a different room. This was a small room, about 10x10, but beautifully appointed, with original hardwood floors and a high ceiling. Plus, its glass doors faced the sand dunes that led to the beach. The sunlight from that door flooded the space.

Incense was burning, a scent that Hallie didn't recognize but was pleasant and calming.

"Frankincense," Willow said. "It has a very calming and clearing scent. I also like to burn sage, as it rids the room of negative energies. But, for your purposes, I think that Frankincense is probably the best. I already burned my sage bundle this morning, so we're good."

Hallie's eyes were drawn to the table in the middle of the room. There was a statue of a beautiful woman with flame in her hands and a cauldron in front of her. Also on the table was a statue of a man with antlers. He had a deer and a bear surrounding him. Her mother had these same statues.

Also on the table were several candles, a chalice, a sword, a wand, and a pentacle, along with three bowls. One decorative bowl had salt in it, another had oil, and another had water. And there was a long rope that was coiled around. There was also a beautiful gold bowl with a small mallet next to it.

On some level, she knew just what all this was for. Still, she had to ask.

"This is an altar," Willow said. "It's where I perform my rituals and spells. All of these things you see have a purpose. This athamé," she said, picking up what Hallie thought was a sword, "connects my energy with that of the moon. I use it for protection against negative energies that might come in while I'm meditating."

Hallie nodded her head and looked at the wand. She was afraid to touch anything on the altar because she somehow knew that it wasn't good to mix energies. She also knew she was a ball of negativity, and she didn't want to transfer that to Willow's tools.

"This wand is something I made from an oak branch I found out in the yard. I didn't cut anything off the tree because I would never harm another living being deliberately. But, since the branch was already on the ground, I took it. It's used to direct and harness energy from the moon, the sun and the heavens. And I use it to draw a protective circle for my rituals."

"A protective circle?"

"Yes. When I perform my rituals and spells, I enter a sacred space, an overlap of the material world and the divine. I use this wand to draw it."

Hallie then looked at the two statues.

"Goddess Brigid," Willow said, pointing to the female statue. "The Celtic goddess of fire, blacksmithing, poetry and the arts and healing. And this dude over here is the god of the underworld and wild animals. His name is Cernunnos. The moon is female, the sun is male. The darkness and the night is female, the wind and daytime is male."

Then Willow explained everything about the items on the altar. Hallie listened to her talk about how some things were used for purification, others were used for harnessing positive energy while expelling negative vibrations, while still others represented the elements of earth, fire, water, air and spirit.

"Anyhow, now that you have a rudimentary knowledge of how things work, I'd like to get into a healing ritual with you. I like to borrow healing techniques from other cultures. I never want to be so arrogant as to believe that other parts of the world don't have knowledge that would be helpful to me in my healing practice. Once I decided to become a healer, I knew that I had to expand my horizons. So, I spent a year at an Ashram in India, where I learned how to do energy cleansing."

"Okay," Hallie said. "Let's try it. I mean, it couldn't hurt."

"No, it won't hurt. And it'll definitely help. So, let's begin."

Chapter Twenty-One

Willow

While Willow knew that Hallie most likely had issues with all of her chakras, she would have to take her healing process one chakra at a time. It would take a while for her new friend to open up to her gifts and become one with the universe. This was because opening up those chakras connected to the cosmos and the divine were typically tackled last.

So, she decided to start with Hallie's root and work her way up. Before Hallie could have her divine energy unblocked, she had to have her root energy flowing freely. Then work her way up, clearing all the others until she got to her crown chakra and soul star chakra, both of which needed to be open for Hallie to receive the energy of the universe and divine.

Willow got two mats, put them down on the floor, and then blew out her Frankincense incense and burned Cedarwood. She got out the Tarot card that represented The

World and handed it to Hallie. "Look at this card and then close your eyes. I want you to absorb the energy of this card. Then I want you to visualize something that creates a safe space for you. Whenever you've felt safe, why did you? What person in your life creates safety for you? Visualize that person and feel that feeling of security."

Willow sat next to Hallie and she, too, closed her eyes. She could sense Hallie relaxing as she meditated. Willow could actually feel her friend's negative energy becoming unbound.

"Now, I asked you to bring a cloth that means something to you. What did you bring?"

Hallie brought out a small cloth that was dark blue with gold stitching. "This. It's a part of the altar covering that my mother used when I was a child. I have another one at home that's intact, so I didn't mind cutting this piece away."

Willow took the cloth and placed some crystals in it. "Black Tourmaline protects you and your property. Jet is also protective and can remove a curse or hex that might've been put on you or one of your lifetimes. Onyx helps you become physically stronger and attracts good luck. Red Aventurine helps clear out stored trauma and strengthens your circulation. It also helps clear out stored toxins and improves your blood flow. Red Jasper strengthens you and makes you more of a badass."

Then Willow took a piece of her own collection of sea glass and placed it in the bundle as well. "This piece of glass has been battered by the ocean and potentially came from lands far away. It survived the battering, just as you will."

Then she took some burning sage and a large crystal wand and waved them over the crystals and the sea glass. She whispered a prayer - "In the divine name of the goddess Brigid, I consecrate and charge these stones as magical tools for healing." And then she tied the cloth up with a bow and blew on it. "With this breath of life, I give thanks to the goddess for this medicine."

Willow imagined a white light surrounding the bundle and then a healing green light surrounding Hallie. She handed Hallie the bundle. "Now, keep this in a safe space in your home. I'll be making other bundles as we work our way up through the rest of the energy centers. This is a group of stones that'll help you feel physically stronger and more secure."

And then Willow got up and made a tea made of cloves, rosemary and allspice. "Rosemary uplifts your spirit. Allspice is healing, increases positive energy and brings good luck. Cloves are associated with protection, healing and purification."

Hallie drank the tea and handed the cup back to Willow. "Thank you."

"Now, how do you feel?"

"Uh, I feel lighter somehow. And yet more grounded. Like I can feel my feet on the floor, and it seems like I belong in this world a bit more."

Willow nodded approvingly. "Okay, let's work through the rest of your energy centers."

For the rest of the afternoon, Willow and Hallie worked through meditation and addressing different healing goddesses. For each of the chakras, Willow created a different crystal bundle and tea at the end of their exercises. And, all the while, Willow was imagining bringing black negative energy out of Hallie and injecting white and green healing energy in the areas where these bad energies were drawn from.

By the time the two were done, Hallie looked like she

was feeling better. And she looked as if she was willing to go on.

And then she started to cry.

Willow knew that this was actually a good thing. She likened the cathartic release of emotions to lancing a boil. You have to get rid of all the infection and gunk that is trapped below the surface, and that means that you need to go through the pain associated with the lancing procedure. Hallie obviously needed to let those emotions flow freely. Now that she was becoming unblocked, those negative memories, hurt, betrayals and unbearable pain were at the surface. She was tapping into it and letting it go.

Willow picked up her oak wand and pointed it at Hallie. "Sacred wand absorb all of Hallie's pain and hurts. Absorb it so that it may be scattered to the universe." As she pointed the wand at Hallie, she imagined black energy leaving Hallie's body and being drawn entirely into the oak wand. As Hallie continued to wail, her face became blotchy and covered completely with tears. Willow continued to chant and point and visualize.

This went on for the next few hours. Hallie would calm down, drink some tea and finger some of the stones that Willow gave her. Willow would ask her to do some visualization, and then the process would start all over again.

By the end of the session, it was completely dark outside. The two women had been working with Hallie's energy for the past twelve hours, and it was now 2 in the morning. The moon was high in the sky.

"Let's go outside," Willow said to Hallie. "Let's look at the moon and give thanks to the goddess for working with us and helping us to heal your soul."

And the unspoken words were that the two women were

going to end up at the beach. Willow always rejuvenated herself when she listened to the tide rolling in and out.

They got to the beach, and Hallie breathed in the night air. "I feel better," she said. "Let's keep doing these rituals, okay? If we do this, along with the acupuncture, I think it will help my healing quite a lot."

"That's the point," Willow said. She was worried about Hallie.

But, when Hallie turned to her in the moonlight, and Willow looked in her eyes she knew Hallie was going to make it.

And that made her smile.

Chapter Twenty-Two

Hallie

For the next several weeks, Hallie continued to receive chemotherapy once a week. She started losing her hair, so she decided to go ahead and shave it all off before it all started going down the drain. And she continued to feel weak as a kitten.

But that cannabis was really helping her with her appetite and her nausea, so she kept taking that. She even went to Sebastian's cooking studio in the historic district several times for private lessons. She was really learning everything she needed to know to make her own delicious meals and treats with cannabis.

And, while she had fantasized the bit about Sebastian when he came to make her and everybody dinner, she found out he had a beautiful girlfriend. His girlfriend, Angelina, was much younger than him. She figured he was in his early 50s, and Angelina appear to be in her early 30s. Angelina was also a chef, and she was his partner at the cooking studio. Angelina was usually there for Hallie's lessons with Sebastian.

It was just as well, as Hallie didn't believe she would have had a chance with Sebastian anyhow. And she was happy to be learning everything she could from Sebastian. She didn't need a relationship at that moment, anyhow. She didn't have the bandwidth for something like that.

She was still working with Willow, both with acupuncture and chakra cleansing. All that helped her immensely, and she was feeling better and stronger every day.

Another thing she was doing, when she had the energy, was working with Charlotte. She found Charlotte had two goals in her life. One goal was to find a career she was happy with and she could work around childcare. She didn't want to have to put Siobhan in any kind of a daycare facility, so she and Charlotte spent their time together researching online every available art writing opportunity on the internet.

But, she also found out that Charlotte had the goal of getting back with her husband. Charlotte felt Siobhan should have a two-parent household. And she also felt there was the possibility that she and Matthew could make it work.

That goal was a bit more challenging for Hallie. But she really worked with Charlotte to uncover exactly why her marriage broke down. At first, Charlotte never wanted to admit she had any role in the breakdown. She told Hallie that she was completely not at fault, and that Matthew was a selfish prig. She asked Hallie how she could make Matthew change. And Hallie told her honestly it wasn't going to happen.

"He's not going to change," Hallie said. "That's the first

thing you have to understand. So, knowing he's not going to change, how can we work together to maybe change your beliefs about the marriage so that the two of you can find common ground?"

Charlotte shook her head. "He has to completely change. He has to only spend time with me and Siobhan when he isn't working. Otherwise, it's not going to work. He can't have any kind of free time. Especially if I'm going to be working, too. The two of us have to focus on Siobhan, and that's that."

Hallie sighed. If there was one thing she knew, it was that everybody had a blind spot when it comes to relationships. She already knew Charlotte's blind spot, and that was that Charlotte was too rigid. Everybody needed a little bit of freedom. Nobody wanted to feel they were put into a cage. The feeling that both parents had to focus on a child to the exclusion of everything else was not only unrealistic, but also unhealthy.

She was going to have to work with Charlotte, little by little, to make her understand this. And that was Hallie's goal for her life coaching with Charlotte.

She had to make Charlotte understand that a successful marriage involved compromises. As much as Charlotte was "her way or the highway," she had to get out of that mindset issue if she ever hoped to make it work with her husband.

Matthew certainly was not blameless. He could have handled things differently. But Charlotte wasn't blameless, either, no matter how much she tried to protest otherwise.

"Okay, Charlotte. Here's what I want you to do. I want you to visualize a life like what you want. A life where you and Matthew don't have other friends, don't have individual hobbies, don't have any downtime from one another. I want you to journal about it. And then let's meet here next week, and talk about what you came up with. And then I want you to journal about some hobbies and passions you have that have nothing to do with your family. And then do the same thing for Matthew. And maybe a journal about how the two of you can fit-"

Charlotte shook her head. "No. It's not gonna work. I mean, I do want to have a job, but the two of us can't have outside interests besides our jobs and Siobhan and making the family work."

Hallie was patient. "Just journal about the alternative life, please. That's what I ask of you for this week."

Charlotte was a challenge, of course. But, Hallie was happy.

Maybe getting Charlotte to see another way of living was a challenge, but it was taking her mind off of her cancer and chemotherapy, and that was important.

For that reason, she looked forward to seeing Charlotte every week.

Chapter Twenty-Three

Charlotte

Charlotte took her sessions with Hallie to heart and knew she had to get her life on track.

She took a deep breath as she saw that a Conrad Maxwell, a local artist with a studio in the historic district, was looking for a ghost-writer for a series of historical novels he was self-publishing under his name.

Charlotte cocked her head and looked on Amazon to see if he had published other novels and saw that he had. He had done quite well for himself, as the books he had published had thousands of 4 and 5-star reviews. All of the novels were what was known as biographical fiction. This genre was centered around a real person, such as a famous artist or writer or somebody like Charles Lindbergh, and then writing a novel about that person.

Charlotte always enjoyed that fiction genre and thought she could do well with it. She'd read many novels in the genre already. The subjects she read about ranged from

Ernest Hemingway to Virginia Woolf to Michelangelo to Beethoven to the old Hollywood actress Hedy Lamarr to several novels about Picasso and several about Vincent Van Gogh. The books about Van Gogh were some of her favorites.

Okay, I have my work cut out for me. She would somehow read at least a couple of these novels before she tried to pursue the ghost-writing position with this guy.

For the rest of that day, Charlotte read books Conrad had produced, in between playing with Siobhan, feeding her, rocking her, and reading to her. She read Conrad's books aloud to Siobhan instead of the usual *Goodnight Moon*-type books she usually read to the little girl. After all, the baby was less than a year old, and she wouldn't know what Charlotte was reading to her, so she might as well read her daughter something that was stimulating to her.

A week later, Charlotte had read 4 of Conrad's books, cover to cover, making notes about how he constructed them, his favorite topics, his writing voice, and how he weaved historical details into the plot.

She was ready to ask Matthew to introduce her to Willow. From there, she hoped to meet with Conrad and impress him with her knowledge of his books, her body of writing work and her mastery of the lives of various artists.

If she could do all that, she might get the ghost-writing job. Conrad was unusually generous to his ghost-writers, as he was offering 50% of net sales, which could add up to quite a bit since his novels sold well. He also offered something of an advance - $5,000 - which meant she didn't have to wait until publication to be paid.

However, fate stepped in before she got a chance to call Matthew. She happened to notice on the dining table downstairs a card. It was a business card for her mother's best friend, Hallie. It was a beautiful painting of a colorful shore with an even more colorful sky. The card said, "Hallie Gleason, assistant manager, Willow Tree Spa."

All at once, Charlotte knew why Willow's name sounded so familiar. She remembered now that Hallie worked for a young psychic named Willow. She went to find her mother.

"Mom, what is Willow's last name? The Willow Hallie works for?" she asked her mother.

"Killeen," Ava said. "Same as your husband. Isn't that funny, now that I think of it. Why do you ask?"

Was it fate? Was something finally going to go right for her?

"I need to make an appointment with Willow. I feel she might be able to help me out with what I want to do."

"Okay," Ava said, looking confused. "Maybe you should, at that. That girl's pretty amazing. She helped Quinn find her daughter when she went missing from the beach, and she helped Hallie find the courage to leave her husband. Maybe she can help you, too."

Charlotte didn't think that she needed psychic help, necessarily, but then again, maybe it wouldn't hurt.

Charlotte called Willow's spa and was informed there was a cancellation. It did seem that fate was smiling at her on this.

It seemed things were falling into place for her. She just had a great feeling that Willow would help her get a job.

Chapter Twenty-Four

Charlotte

Charlotte took her sessions with Hallie to heart and knew she had to get her life on track.

She took a deep breath as she saw that a Conrad Maxwell, a local artist with a studio in the historic district, was looking for a ghost-writer for a series of historical novels he was self-publishing under his name.

Charlotte cocked her head and looked on Amazon to see if he had published other novels and saw that he had. He had done quite well for himself, as the books he had published had thousands of 4 and 5-star reviews. All of the novels were what was known as biographical fiction. This genre was centered around a real person, such as a famous artist or writer or somebody like Charles Lindbergh, and then writing a novel about that person.

Charlotte always enjoyed that fiction genre and thought she could do well with it. She'd read many novels in the genre already. The subjects she read about ranged from

Ernest Hemingway to Virginia Woolf to Michelangelo to Beethoven to the old Hollywood actress Hedy Lamarr to several novels about Picasso and several about Vincent Van Gogh. The books about Van Gogh were some of her favorites.

Okay, I have my work cut out for me. She would somehow read at least a couple of these novels before she tried to pursue the ghost-writing position with this guy.

For the rest of that day, Charlotte read books Conrad had produced, in between playing with Siobhan, feeding her, rocking her, and reading to her. She read Conrad's books aloud to Siobhan instead of the usual *Goodnight Moon*-type books she usually read to the little girl. After all, the baby was less than a year old, and she wouldn't know what Charlotte was reading to her, so she might as well read her daughter something that was stimulating to her.

A week later, Charlotte had read 4 of Conrad's books, cover to cover, making notes about how he constructed them, his favorite topics, his writing voice, and how he weaved historical details into the plot.

She was ready to ask Matthew to introduce her to Willow. From there, she hoped to meet with Conrad and impress him with her knowledge of his books, her body of writing work and her mastery of the lives of various artists.

If she could do all that, she might get the ghost-writing job. Conrad was unusually generous to his ghost-writers, as he was offering 50% of net sales, which could add up to quite a bit since his novels sold well. He also offered something of an advance - $5,000 - which meant she didn't have to wait until publication to be paid.

However, fate stepped in before she got a chance to call Matthew. She happened to notice on the dining table downstairs a card. It was a business card for her mother's best friend, Hallie. It was a beautiful painting of a colorful shore with an even more colorful sky. The card said, "Hallie Gleason, assistant manager, Willow Tree Spa."

All at once, Charlotte knew why Willow's name sounded so familiar. She remembered now that Hallie worked for a young psychic named Willow. She went to find her mother.

"Mom, what is Willow's last name? The Willow Hallie works for?" she asked her mother.

"Killeen," Ava said. "Same as your husband. Isn't that funny, now that I think of it. Why do you ask?"

Was it fate? Was something finally going to go right for her?

"I need to make an appointment with Willow. I feel she might be able to help me out with what I want to do."

"Okay," Ava said, looking confused. "Maybe you should, at that. That girl's pretty amazing. She helped Quinn find her daughter when she went missing from the beach, and she helped Hallie find the courage to leave her husband. Maybe she can help you, too."

Charlotte didn't think that she needed psychic help, necessarily, but then again, maybe it wouldn't hurt.

Charlotte called Willow's spa and was informed there was a cancellation. It did seem that fate was smiling at her on this.

It seemed things were falling into place for her. She just had a great feeling that Willow would help her get a job.

Chapter Twenty-Five

Sarah

Sarah went through the entire process of getting her coin at auction at Sotheby's. She submitted it to the auctioneers, along with the certificate from the PGCS people. There was a private viewing, and the coin was due to be bid on in one week.

She was very nervous about it. She had no idea what to expect. She had no clue if it would fetch $50,000 or much more. She had a pretty good feeling the coin would get at least $50,000, though. That seemed to be the bottom price for this particular coin.

Ava was going to go to the auction with her in New York. "I am just as excited as you are about this," Ava said. "I'm dying to find out how much that coin is worth."

Sarah just shrugged her shoulders, trying to downplay the whole thing. "Maybe it'll be enough for me to put a down payment on a house, although I doubt it."

She had allowed herself to dream, however. For the past

few evenings, she looked online at houses for sale around the island. There was one she toured that she absolutely fell in love with. It wasn't big - it was only a two-bedroom. But it was close to the Miacomet beach. And it was a fixer-upper, so it was priced low for the area −$1 million.

But it had good bones. That's what Sarah was looking for. It didn't matter what kind of cosmetic issues it had. And it had quite a few of those – the floors had seen better days, the kitchen was extremely dated, as were the bathrooms. But Sarah saw the potential in the house, and there was something about the house that spoke to her. She was drawn to it like she had not been drawn to any other house.

It was her house. She just had to make enough money at auction to put 20% down on the home, which would be $200,000. That number had always seemed out of reach to her before. And it still felt that way. Sarah definitely wouldn't count her chickens before they hatched.

Quinn drove Ava and Sarah to the airport. "Hallie wasn't feeling well. Otherwise, she would be coming to the airport with you guys," Quinn explained. "I worry about her."

Hallie had been having some problems with the chemo-therapy. She was currently battling an infection, which complicated matters greatly. The good thing was that she could make her own cannabis brownies and cannabis food when she needed it. Sarah knew Hallie was trying not to become dependent upon it, but sometimes you had to do what you had to do to keep up your strength.

"She'll be okay," Sarah said. "She has to be."

Sarah and Ava got to the puddle jumper airport, where they would fly to Boston and then fly on to New York City. Once they got to New York City, they would check in at The Benjamin Hotel, an old school hotel little over a mile away from the auction house. Sarah was footing the bill for all of this, and it was costing her a mint. The hotel alone was almost $600 a night, and the plane tickets were costing her a grand apiece round-trip.

She certainly hoped this trip would be worth her while. Otherwise, it would just be another $4,000 or so coming out of her pocket for no reason.

A few hours later, the ladies were checked in at The Benjamin. This was a beautiful hotel located in one of the historic buildings from the 1800s. There was a bellhop outside greeting them, and Sarah and Ava walked across the beautifully tiled floor to the front desk and checked in.

After they checked in, they went to the rooftop terrace and had a glass of wine. "Are you nervous?" Ava asked Sarah as they took in the city scenes. It was now the middle of October. The crisp autumn air brought Sarah back to some happy memories that usually took place around October. Fall was always her favorite time of year. She loved the changing of the season, how summer was slowly transitioning into the colder months. It was already sweater weather, and she could imagine bonfires and fireplaces blazing to warm up bodies getting colder by the day.

She knew she had to go to Central Park before returning to Nantucket. Central Park would be ablaze in the season's colors, and she was looking forward to walking along the paths and kicking the leaves.

"I am nervous," she said to Ava. "I just don't know what's going to happen. Maybe it'll do well, maybe it won't."

"What are you going to do once the auction goes through? Are you going to try to find Olivia and talk to her?"

"Of course. That's one of the first things I'm going to do. I had to satisfy my curiosity about why she would send it to me and why she would do it the way she did. Why just send me the penny without telling me what it is? Without even telling me who sent it? What if I would've gotten the penny and got insulted and just threw it away? She was taking a chance that I would've done that. Yes, I'm definitely going to see her to see just what she was thinking of."

The ladies went down to the restaurant to have a meal. After that, Sarah felt tired, so they went back to their room, climbed into their pajamas, and found something to watch on Netflix. Sarah didn't really care what they watched. She knew she would just fall asleep in front of the television anyway.

And so she did.

Chapter Twenty-Six

Sarah

The next day, Ava and Sarah went to the auction house. Sarah was fascinated by some of the works of art and coins and stamps that were being auctioned off that day. And she was even more astounded by some of the prices people were paying for things. For instance, a painting by the artist Basquiat went for over $100 million. Some Chippendale furniture sold for over $100,000.

And then it came to her coin. The auctioneer started the bidding at $50,000, and somebody immediately put his paddle up for that. The auctioneer went up from there.

At first, it seemed different people were putting their paddles up. But, after a little while, it was obvious that the bidding was between two different guys.

Ava nudged Sarah. Then she whispered, "I know both of these guys. They're both billionaires who are avid coin collectors. I remember reading about them in the paper."

Sarah looked from one guy to the next. The bidding was

now at over $1 million, and it looked like both of these guys were determined they were going to win. Sarah was holding her breath. Was this really happening? Was she really going to come out of this with more money than she ever dreamed of having on her own? And all because of a penny?

It was astounding. Simply astounding.

Obviously, these two billionaires would not let the other person have the penny. Every time the auctioneer said a figure, one of the two billionaires would put the paddle up. The other would put his paddle up with the next figure.

It was over $2 million at this point. The previous record was $1.7 million in 2010. It seemed there was no stopping any of this. Each of the two billionaires was determined to have her penny.

Sarah felt she was floating on air as the auctioneer finally announced that her penny was sold at $2.75 million. She shook her head. The auctioneer moved on to the next item, a painting by an artist Sarah didn't know. But, by then, she wasn't listening. All she knew was she was rich. She would be able to buy her own home.

She would just have to wait for a check from Sotheby's. They would take their 10% commission, the PGCS people would get 1%, and she would have to pay taxes on the money, of course. But after everything was said and done, she figured she would have almost $1.5 million to put on a house.

Ava and Sarah left, and they got into their Uber. "Oh my God," Ava said. "What just happened? Did that just happen? It's like the craziest thing ever. Did you ever think it would go up to that amount of money?"

Sarah shook her head. And then she looked at her

phone to see if she could discern why these two billionaires wanted that penny so much.

There was already an article on Google about the auction. The article stated that a billionaire by the name of Lance McGregor was the one who won the auction. Apparently, Mr. McGregor had two other 1943 copper pennies at home and had been looking for the 1943–D one ever since. Sarah's penny, which was from the Denver mint, was the rarest of all the 1943 copper pennies. The other billionaire going against him, Walter Reynolds, also had been looking for the 1943 –D copper penny. That was the reason why the auction went so crazy. Two men were determined to have the coin, and both men had money to burn. She was surprised the auction didn't go to $10 million with that set of facts.

Sarah just smiled. "I know both of us have had our problems with wealthy men. I was dating one for many years, and he was really a jerk to me. You represented many of them, and they were jerks to you. But, on this day, at this hour, I'm grateful for rich guys who have the money to waste on something as insignificant as a copper penny."

Ava smiled back. "I don't blame you. I don't blame you one bit."

Chapter Twenty-Seven

Sarah

The first thing Sarah did after she got the money from her auction was send Lucas in San Diego $28,000. She promised him she would send him 1% of the sell price, and she was as good as her word. He was the first person to confirm to her she had something valuable, and that meant a lot to her.

The second thing she did was book a flight to Nice. The beautiful French city was nestled at the foot of the Italian alps and was bordered by the Mediterranean Sea. The scenic city had its roots in antiquity, as the ancient Greeks called the place Nike, after the goddess Nike. Since that time, the city had gone to the country of Savoy, then to France, then to Italy, and back to France. Through it all, the architecture reflected the diversity of the countries that claimed the city throughout the years. During the latter part of the 1800s, the Gilded Age, the English upper classes started building their summer homes, attracted as they were to the mild Mediterranean climate and the beautiful views of both the Alps and the Mediterranean Sea.

Sarah loved this city. She had visited it quite a few times over the years with Nolan. She had traveled all over the corners of France, from the lovely towns nestled in the mountains to the coastal cities and beyond. Of all the places in France, though, Nice was one of her favorites.

As much as she wanted to do her usual sightseeing - she could never get enough of touristy destinations, no matter how many times she visited a locale - she wasn't there to visit tourist traps.

She was there for a very specific purpose - to see Olivia Shea. Olivia never did change her last name because she never divorced Nolan, and she never married her longtime boyfriend, Gabriel, even though Nolan had passed away and Olivia was free to do what she wanted. All that was a mystery to Sarah. It made her curious, but not as curious as to why Olivia chose to send Sarah such a valuable coin in the mail without even letting her know what it was.

She had tracked Olivia's exact address down through Nolan's address book that she still had in her possession. She hoped the woman still lived in the same place she used to. Otherwise, Sarah was making this trip for no reason.

Well, not for no reason, exactly. It would still be worth it to visit this beautiful city even if she never found Olivia. But she would be very disappointed if Olivia was no longer around.

She got to Olivia's home, marched on up, and rang the doorbell. The home was an Italianate mansion on a cliff overlooking the sea. She imagined a butler or somebody would answer the door, but no. Olivia herself came to the door.

Olivia was smaller than Sarah had imagined in her head. She'd never seen a picture of her because Nolan didn't keep photos of the two of them. She was as beautiful as Sarah had imagined, however. The woman was only around 5'2" and probably didn't weigh much more than 100 lbs or so. Her dark hair was wavy and went halfway down her back, her beautiful brown eyes were large and fringed by long eyelashes, and her nose was strong and Roman. Her lips were a bit thin, but they looked right on her somehow.

Her body was muscular and taut. She was wearing a negligee, and her feet were bare. She had a drink in her hand that smelled of liquor, even though it was in the early afternoon.

She cocked her head. "Sarah," she said. "I was expecting you. That auction went well, didn't it?"

Now, Sarah felt uncomfortable. Of course, this woman would know who she was. She felt Olivia had been keeping tabs on her for quite a while, even if Sarah didn't return the favor.

"I'm sorry," Sarah said. "I don't know what to say. You threw me off guard."

She smiled. "Come in, come in," she said. "Gabriel is around somewhere, I think. Or maybe not. Who knows? But come in."

She padded through her palatial home in her bare feet while Sarah followed her through the elegant mansion with the spare white walls, white furniture, floor-to-ceiling windows and luxury appointments such as the baby grand piano in the corner of one of the rooms.

"Do you play?" Olivia asked Sarah as she saw Sarah eyeing the piano.

"No," Sarah said. "I don't."

"Oh, neither do I. Neither does Gabriel, for that matter.

We just have the piano because we love to entertain, and a lot of our guests like to sit down to the piano and light it up like a Christmas tree. Are you staying for any length of time? If you are, we're having a party this Saturday night. Everyone will be here. If you're in town, you'll come too, okay?"

Sarah took a deep breath. She still felt off-balance because this woman was chatting away at her as if she and Sarah were old friends, when it was the opposite. Sarah had only ever heard her name before, and was never even able to put a face to the name.

Olivia wound her way to an enormous concrete terrace, where she sat down on one of the lounger chairs and lit up a cigarette. Sarah smiled as she remembered that people still smoked in France. It had been so long since she'd seen somebody smoke a cigarette in front of her, she'd forgotten what a cigarette even smelled like.

Olivia offered Sarah one of her cigarettes, but Sarah waved it away. Olivia just shrugged and inhaled some smoke and let it out in one long tendril. "So, you followed all the clues, and it led you to where I wanted you to go. Good for you. I was excited to read about the auction. $2.75 million! It went for more than I thought."

"How much did you think it would go for?"

"Oh, I thought it would sell for at least $2 million, but I thought it would be more than that. I knew two billionaires in New York City were hot for that coin, and I knew they would be going against one another. I wish I could've been a fly on the wall during that auction. Talk about exciting! Did you get tingles crawling up your leg just sitting there, waiting to see how much of a millionaire you would end up? I hope so. I get tingles in my leg just thinking about it."

"Okay," Sarah said. "Let's back up. Why did you send that to me?"

"Oh, I wanted you to have something. Nolan left me everything, as you know. And that's because he was a silly, prideful, arrogant man who thought he was invincible and would live forever. Even when he had a disease that kills almost everyone in two years time, he still thought he would go on living like some kind of immortal god or something like that. He suffered from hubris, which was always the undoing for any mortal in a Greek tragedy."

Sarah nodded her head. "Yes, he certainly was hubristic."

"Right. He should've made a will. Believe it or not, I called him and told him to make a will after I discovered he had ALS. I didn't want his fortune. I didn't deserve it. He set me up in this beautiful home with all the money I could ever want, but I never wanted that, either. I like to work for what I have. It's no good otherwise."

Sarah didn't know Olivia called Nolan about making a will. "What did Nolan tell you when you called him about making a will?"

"He said he would get around to it. I told him he better. I didn't want him to leave it all to you, though. I wanted him to leave his billions to charity. I wanted him to leave you at least a couple of million, though. Listen, I don't think I need to tell you how much inheriting billions can warp your brain and sense of reality. It's no good for anyone. Did you ever read about some of the children of the gilded age tycoons like Cornelius Vanderbilt?"

Sarah actually had read about Cornelius Vanderbilt's children. His son, also named Cornelius, and nicknamed "Corneel", was in and out of mental institutions, was deeply in debt because of gambling and prostitutes and killed himself at 53. His other son, Billy, inherited all the money and wasn't much happier.

"Yes," Sarah said. "But Corneel was epileptic, which caused a lot of his issues."

"Well, true. But, trust me, I've read many biographies of great men who made fortunes, and most of their kids fared poorly, to say the least. There's something to inheriting great wealth that messes with your head. Anyhow, I wanted you to have a few million of Nolan's money, but no more than that. I figure a few million would be enough to set you up so you can do whatever you wanted to do with your life, but not so much that you're freaked out and scared somebody might kidnap you for ransom."

"So, what happened when you inherited the wealth?"

"Oh, I gave it away," Olivia said with a wave of her hand. "All of it. I gave it to homeless people shelters and homeless animal shelters all over Europe. I formed a foundation with the money, and all of the money has been distributed already. Which is what I wanted Nolan to do, anyhow."

Sarah cocked her head. "And the penny?"

"Yes, the penny. Well, I wanted you to have some money. But, you know, I didn't want to pay the gift tax on it. I'd have to pay almost 50% tax if I wanted to send you straight money through your bank account or through a check. Then I thought about it. I kept that penny all these years because it fascinated me. The romance of it all - just 20 pennies like it in the world! Then I came up with a brilliant idea. I would send you the penny in the mail without any kind of letter with it to explain what it was. If the French authorities come after me, I would just say I sent you one penny and nothing more. How did I know it was a valuable penny?" She shrugged her shoulders. "Maybe it was just an ordinary penny. I could tell the authorities I sent the penny to you as an insult. Play dumb. How could they prove I knew better?"

"Would that work?"

"Sure, it would work. It already has. My accountant told me I was in the clear. The French authorities don't know about the penny, anyhow. And they never will. I just wanted to cover my tracks by sending it to you without explanation."

Sarah cocked her head. "Wow. I guess I have my explanation for all this. And thank you. I can't tell you how much that penny has changed my life."

"That's what I wanted to hear," Olivia said. "Really, that made my day. I felt for you, spending so many years with such a lame guy as Nolan and walking away with nothing. And now you have something. Not a ton. That money won't go far once you buy a house and fix it up on the island where you're living. Trust me on that. But it'll give you breathing room and a home of your own. What could be better than that? Enjoy it. Enjoy it."

Sarah shook Olivia's hand. "Thanks again," she said. "I really need to be getting back to my life on the island. There's a house waiting there for me. It's my house. I haven't bid on it yet, but I will as soon as I get back. But that house was made for me. And I, for it. But I literally couldn't do it without you."

She smiled. "You would've gotten there sooner or later. I just gave you a rocket boost. That's all. Now, are you going to stay for my party? You can meet lots of interesting people. Lots of men. Or women, if you're into that."

"Thanks for the offer, but I have to get back."

"Okay. Well, don't be a stranger. If you happen to get to

this part of the world again, please stop by. You're always welcome."

Sarah walked away from that mansion with a smile on her face. She not only had the money to buy a home, but she'd apparently made a new friend.

What could be better than that?

Chapter Twenty-Eight

Charlotte

Two weeks after meeting Willow, Charlotte had her meeting with Conrad. She asked Willow to go with her to break the ice, and the young psychic agreed. "Yeah, it's probably a good idea I go along. Conrad gets weird meeting new peeps sometimes. He'll feel more comfortable being introduced to you by a friendly face."

The two girls got to Conrad's studio, which was in the historic district and housed in an enormous Cape Cod home painted blue with white shutters. Inside the house were several different photography and art studios. Conrad's was on the top floor and featured a skylight, new hardwood floors, floor-to-ceiling windows and overhead track lighting. All around the studio were paintings and sculptures.

Charlotte saw that Conrad's work combined surrealism with Dadaism, with a healthy dose of protest art.

"Dude, I found your new ghostwriter," Willow said as the girls entered his studio. "This is Charlotte Killeen. She's married to my loser cousin Matthew, but she's not like him. And she's one helluva writer."

"Bugger off," Conrad said with a smile. His accent was clearly British. Physically, he wasn't at all how Charlotte had pictured him. With a name like Conrad Maxwell, she imagined him to be broad and blonde, young and American.

In reality, he was skinny, 50ish, with long grey hair tied in a man bun. His blue eyes were sharp, however, and his smile was genuine. "I'm in the middle of a work that's turning out to be shit, yet will be exhibited. People will spit on it unless I can figure out how to save it."

Willow took a look at the painting that Conrad was working on. "Hey, Conrad, tool, you made this appointment. Remember?"

"Right. And I was going to cancel because I'm ass-deep into this project, but time slipped away, and I just forgot."

"Sorry, the world doesn't work that way," Willow said. "You made the appointment with Charlotte, and you're going to keep it."

Conrad sighed. "Oh, all right. But you have to tell me how this piece is coming first."

Willow examined Conrad's painting. "Yeah, you gotta add some color in there somewhere. It doesn't really say 'Conrad Maxwell' to me. It's not signature. Then again, maybe that's good it's not canon. It's different. Take a risk. Forget what I said. Keep it all black and white."

Conrad looked at Charlotte. "What say you?" he asked her. "Would you spit on this painting or buy it and put it on your walls?"

Charlotte felt her heart pounding. He would be looking for an insightful critique from her, and she better deliver.

The painting was that of an African prince, with such detail that it looked photorealistic. However, the face was as if it had been sliced into three different parts. In the sliced parts were other faces, also photorealistic in their detail. One of the faces was a policeman with a KKK hood, a gun and a badge. The other face was a young white girl whose face was screwed up in a rage, her mouth open, her eyes way too big for her face. The third visage was that of a man who apparently was a founding father. He was wearing an enormous white wig, and his mouth was much too large for his face. Behind the chopped-up image of the African prince was a mushroom cloud.

Charlotte started to give a critique that would show she knew what Dadaism and surrealism were. "This picture clearly shows that you're influenced by Tristan Tzara and Hannah Hoch and is a great example of Dadaism in the modern world," she began.

To that, Conrad rolled his eyes. "Blah, blah, blah. You know what Dadaism is. Good for you. You get a gold star. I could give bugger-all about that. That wasn't what I asked you. I asked you if you thought this picture was good or if you would spit on it if you saw it hanging in a gallery opening."

Charlotte looked at the picture and realized it wasn't really her taste. While she could appreciate it for what it was – a protest against African colonialism and slavery and how slavery presents itself in the modern world with hatred and fear - protest art wasn't really what she preferred to hang on her walls. She tended more towards the traditional artists - Monet's delicate flowers, Degas' beautiful ballerinas, Renoir's lush garden parties, Manet's sturdy aristocrats.

This was ironic. Her art history course interests tended more towards the *avant-garde*, mainly because she was interested in the politics behind some of the great works of modern artists. This was why she chose to write her senior honors thesis on Max Ernst, a surrealist artist she certainly wouldn't hang on her walls but who fascinated her nonetheless.

She realized Conrad was looking for an honest answer, so she hit him with it. "It's not my taste. That said, as an example of the kind of art it represents, it's excellent. It's accessible, the meaning is clear, and it has something to say. It'll provoke a visceral reaction in the viewer, which makes art truly great."

Conrad nodded his head. "Yes, a visceral reaction. That's what art truly is, after all. You can know everything there is to know about the great artists of the past and the different genres. But most people who buy art don't know any of that crap, nor do they care. They could give bugger-all about any of it. All they want to know is how it makes them feel. So, I assume you wouldn't put this on your walls?"

Charlotte shook her head. "No, it's not my taste. I'm sorry, my aesthetic preferences are soothing and traditional. Dégas, Monet, Renoir, Manet. The realist and impressionist masters."

"I see. Yet you're interested in Max Ernst's work because I see that this is what you wrote a paper on when you were a pupil. What drew you to him?"

"Well, I'll be honest. I'm drawn to artists who use their artwork to make strong statements about society. Max Ernst was a fascinating study for me because of his background. He was part of the group of artists in occupied France and imprisoned by the Nazis because of their beliefs. I was interested to know how his experience in the concentration camp informed his art. Of course, my interest in that part of his life led me to many other artists experiencing the same thing. In my paper on Max Ernst, you'll see that I included his contemporaries who were also imprisoned because of their beliefs."

Charlotte felt remarkably comfortable around this man. She didn't really know why. He just had a way about him. Of course, she still felt inferior to him because of his talent. But, at the same time, he just seemed to have an ease about him.

He nodded his head. "Willow, what can you tell me about Charlotte here?"

Willow shrugged her shoulders. "I don't know much about her. I just met her. I know she's married to my cousin, which, to be honest with you, speaks very little about her judgment. Not to mention her taste in men. But, I read enough of her undergraduate honors thesis to know she's a great writer. Her writing has a certain sardonic quality you'll appreciate. This chick gets dark. She's not afraid to go there. If you want a ghostwriter who can really dig down into the psyche of the artists you're writing about, she's your woman."

Conrad nodded his head. "High praise. High praise, indeed. Well, I gotta get back to my work. You're hired. Even though I lined up some interviews today, I don't have the energy to talk to anybody else about this. Just the thought of interviewing all these people makes me want to scoop out my eyeballs with a dull knife. But, fair warning, if you cock this up, I'll sack you. But, if you do a good job, I'll have lots of projects for you. I'll keep you busy year-round. As you know, I write historical biographical fiction. Usually, the subject of my novels are artists. My books have all been bestsellers, and they've hit all the lists. I only hire ghost-writers when I get too busy with my art projects to produce books, which I need to produce because I'm desperately low on alcohol and pills, and I need the money from my novels to keep me in the manner to which I've become accustomed."

Charlotte opened her mouth and shut it again.

Conrad winked. "Just kidding about the alcohol and pills thing. Just wanted to stay with the crazy artist stereotype. Don't get me wrong - I love a good glass of Jameson, same as anybody else, but it doesn't consume me. Mainly, I just need a ghostwriter because I want my name always out there with something new all the time, and I just don't have the time for it anymore. So, Charlotte, you've got the job. You can write, and that's all I need to know."

"But you don't need to know how well I can write a novel, though?"

Conrad cocked his head at Willow. "Willow, what say you? What's your feeling about this lass? I trust you because you know things you shouldn't."

"Conrad, I'm getting messages from the universe that Charlotte will write your next bestseller. She's a natural. She just doesn't know it yet."

"Well, there you go," Conrad said. "I'll trust Willow's psychic powers, which haven't ever gone wrong. So, go for it, young Charlotte. I'm interested in Soutine, so find out as much about him as possible. Especially his time living in occupied France and fleeing the Nazis. Bring in the other cast of characters from that time - Chagall, Modigliani, Pascin - and you can put together a cracking good story."

Charlotte felt her heart soar. "Thank you for the opportunity."

He waved his hand at her. "Here's my outline. Hopefully, you can make heads or tails of it. It's not the best. You're going to have to do some of your own research, this outline's shit, but it generally tells you what I'm looking for. In the meantime, sod off. I have to get this done."

Charlotte took the outline and looked over at Willow. She was nodding her head at Charlotte. "I told you, dude. Now, let's get out of here. We gotta leave this guy alone, so he can get this painting done before the showing."

As they drove back to Willow's studio, Charlotte felt like she was floating on air. "I can't believe it was as easy as all that!"

"Easy as all what? Listen, Conrad would hire you no matter what, just because he hates doing that interviewing crap. He just read a few pages of your senior honors thesis and knew you could handle the job. That's all he was looking for. Once he figured out that you could handle it, that was all she wrote. No pun intended."

"Well, then, I owe this job all to you. If you didn't take me to meet him, somebody else would've gotten the job."

"Yeah, I guess so."

"Would you like to go for a drink? I'll buy, of course. I really feel I should do something to thank you for what you just did for me. You didn't even know me, yet you went to bat for me."

She took a deep breath. "Listen, I may say bad things about your husband, my cousin. But, to be honest with you, I think he's pretty cool. I know what he did to you, and I know why. Getting a job like this will probably help things out between you two. That's why I wanted to meet you in the first place. If I read your work, and I didn't think that you were any good, I would've thrown you out on your ass. But I thought your writing and your insights were excellent, so have at it, hoss. You don't owe me a thing. I know it will sound cheesy to say this, but the best way you can repay me is to kick ass on this project and show Matthew what he's missing."

They arrived back at Willow's house, and Charlotte got

out of Willow's car. "Well, again, thank you. I know this sounds really cheesy myself. In fact, I will have to get some good wine to go with this cheese, but I really would like to become friends with you."

Willow shrugged her shoulders. "Sure. Give me a call, and we'll go out and grab a drink."

Charlotte nodded and left.

As she walked to her car, she couldn't believe her good fortune. She got a job! And it was a job that could work around her schedule. Even if she did have to meet with Conrad every week, most of the work for this ghostwriting project would be online, on her schedule, on her terms. It would require a lot of research, but she could take Siobhan to the library, no problem. Most of this job was going to be done right there in her home. Of course, she had to do a great job with it. If she did, she could make this gig a full-time thing.

She felt like she was on her way at last.

But when she walked in the door of the house, she had a most unpleasant surprise. Matthew was there. And he looked frantic.

"Charlotte, we have to get to the hospital. Right now."

Chapter Twenty-Nine

Ava

Ava was watching Siobhan while Charlotte was seeing an artist about a job. Her daughter seemed very excited about this meeting. She'd told her mother all about what Conrad Maxwell was looking for.

But of course, wouldn't you know it, while Charlotte was gone, Siobhan started to spike a fever. She also started to vomit and began to squint at the light in her bedroom above her crib, as if the light was too bright for her. And, when she cried, it was a sound she hadn't made before. It was more of a moan than a cry, a low-pitched guttural growl.

Ava's maternal instincts - that never dulled even some 24 years after giving birth to her children - were kicked into gear. It was almost like she had muscle memory for this kind of thing. She just knew there was something seriously wrong with the little girl. This wasn't just the usual case of a baby spiking a fever and vomiting, a 24-hour bug that would work its way out. No, this was something else. She didn't like how the baby was squinting in the light, she didn't like her cry, and her fever spiked to 103 degrees.

So, she tried to call Charlotte. However, Charlotte apparently had turned off her phone. That was to be expected, considering she was meeting with Willow and, hopefully, Conrad Maxwell. Ava's frustration grew as 15 minutes ticked by, and she still couldn't get a hold of her daughter.

Quinn and Hallie weren't available to help Ava with this matter. Hallie was doing chemo at that time, and Quinn was with her, over Hallie's protests that Quinn had enough going on without sitting there at the chemo center. Quinn finally told her she was going to be with her, no matter what, and Hallie finally gave in. So, both women weren't available to help Ava with Siobhan.

The upshot was that Ava would have to take Siobhan over to the urgent care place, and she was going to have to do it on her own.

But maybe not. Sarah was around, and she ran into Ava on Ava's way out the door.

"What's going on?" she asked her.

Ava shook her head. "I need to take Siobhan over to urgent care. I don't like the way she's looking – do you see how pale she is? I don't like the way she's crying - she sounds strange, hoarse, and it's more like a moan than a cry. She's got a fever, a very high fever, and she's vomiting. And she can't seem to stand the light. Listen, you hold down the fort here, and I'm going to –"

"Just a second, I'll get my coat."

"Get your coat? What do you mean?"

"You haven't seen how the temperature has dropped in the past hour? It's going to storm. And it's going to get cold.

You better wrap up Siobhan. She might get cold too. And you're gonna need your own coat."

Sarah was back in a couple of minutes. "Ava, we don't need to take her to urgent care. We need to take her to the ER. And I mean right now."

"Why?"

"I just punched up the symptoms on my phone on my way to get my coat, and it sounds like meningitis. Urgent Care can't treat that. According to the website that I looked at, if the doctor doesn't catch meningitis quickly, she could have permanent brain damage or worse. So let's go."

Meningitis. Ava had a feeling there was something seriously wrong with her granddaughter.

The two of them hurried out the door and got into Ava's SUV, buckling Siobhan in the back in her car seat.

Ava arrived at the hospital in five minutes. She screeched to a stop in front of the ER, and Sarah hopped out with Siobhan in her arms. "I'll see you after you park the car," she said breathlessly as she walked through the double doors and disappeared into the ER.

Ava said a little prayer after she parked the car, and she joined Sarah in the ER. She and Siobhan were nowhere to be seen, which was a good sign and a bad sign. It was a good sign because Siobhan was getting care immediately. It was also a bad sign because she obviously was so sick that they took her right away.

She told the nurse that her granddaughter was being seen and was told to take a seat. She did and kept trying to call Charlotte.

Forty-five minutes later, Sarah came out and joined her. "They're caring for her," he said. "They suspect bacterial meningitis. They just did a spinal tap. Bacterial meningitis can kill in a hurry. Sometimes it doesn't kill, but it causes mental retardation, deafness, all kinds of permanent disabilities."

"She'll make it through," Ava said, unsure if what she was saying was true.

"Do you know that if it isn't treated, it's 100% fatal? Even when it's treated, they have to get it fast. I hope and pray that we brought her in quick enough."

Ava tried Charlotte's number again, but Charlotte came through the ER door just then. With her were Deacon, Quinn and Hallie.

"Where is she? Where is Siobhan?" Charlotte demanded.

Ava stood up and held her daughter. "The doctors are examining her."

Deacon came over to Ava and put his hand on her shoulder. "You okay? I drove Charlotte here because she was too upset to drive. Then I called Quinn, and she came up here with Hallie. I hope you don't feel like we're ambushing you, mate."

Ava just shook her head. She couldn't speak. She kept hearing Sarah's words about bacterial meningitis. About how it can kill. "Thank you for bringing Charlotte. You don't have to stay, of course. I can drive her home."

"I'd like to stay if it's all the same to you," Deacon said.

Ava couldn't speak. Quinn and Hallie came over to sit next to her.

Hallie and Quinn sat next to Ava, one on each side of her. "Sugar, she'll pull through," Quinn said. "Have faith."

"Faith." Ava took a deep breath. "Faith." Ava hadn't had faith in much of anything for a long, long time. She wished she did, but life just seemed to beat her down. Every time she felt like she was turning a corner, something else came along and snapped her right back. Her life had been such a roller-coaster for the past few years. She felt like she was whip-lashed.

Just then, Matthew came in the door of the hospital. "Believe it or not, I was already on the island. I was here because I wanted to ask Charlotte to possibly give me another chance. I was with Charlotte when she got the call about Siobhan. Is she okay?"

Matthew was there. Ava was feeling an even greater sense of whiplash at that moment. "You're here? I don't understand. What caused you to want to come here?"

"I told you. Ava, I've been having a lot of second thoughts about Charlotte and my daughter lately. And I really want to ask her to come back to me. I understand things are really screwed up between the two of us, but I want to try to make things right."

Ava put her hand to her mouth. She was thinking that not only was Matthew going to have to make nice with Charlotte, but Charlotte was going to have to do the same thing for him. After all, she was the one who was under-handed in the whole situation. She was the one who didn't take her birth control pills for months, not telling Matthew that was the case. Maybe Ava was overthinking it. Perhaps it wasn't necessary to tell him the truth. But, she realized one thing when her mother kept secrets from her. Secrets always come out, one way or another. And the longer it takes for the secrets to come out, the worse it is when they actually do come out.

Ava looked over at Matthew, who was trying to get close to Charlotte, but she didn't seem to be having it. Ava watched her daughter refuse Matthew's hand. And then Charlotte stood up and raised her voice. "Don't touch me, you jerk. You never wanted her. Well, guess what? You might get your wish, after all! You might get your wish, after all!"

Everybody in the ER looked at Charlotte, who was screaming like a madwoman. Ava rapidly walked over to her daughter and put her arms around her. "Don't punish him like that," Ava said. "He's hurting, too. I know that you don't believe that, but-"

"Hurting? What are you talking about? This is what he wants." She pointed at Matthew, who was very pale. His eyes were red-rimmed, and his expression was that of an inconsolable man. "He'd love it if Siobhan would die. That would mean that he can continue his life as a single guy. He'll never have to worry about paying child support, and he'll never have to explain to every woman he meets that he has this baggage by the name of Siobhan. He can just pretend Siobhan and me never even happened. He can erase both of us now."

Matthew didn't say a word to defend himself. Ava imagined he was beating himself up just as much as Charlotte was beating on him.

Ava had to get away from that room. She felt like she was suffocating. "I'm going to find a vending machine," she said. "I'll bring back treats for everyone." She didn't take orders like she usually would. She didn't have the energy to ask anybody else what they wanted, and she didn't have the mental capacity to remember anyhow.

She walked down the hallway, and Deacon caught up with her. "Is there anything I can do for you?" he asked her.

Ava just shook her head. She had to keep it together. Everyone around her was falling apart, so she needed to be the lynchpin that kept everyone else sane. "No," she said. "I just need to somehow comfort Matthew and Charlotte because they both need a sympathetic ear. But Charlotte can't hear that Matthew is hurting, and Matthew can't reach out to Charlotte because he knows how angry she is with him. If I know my daughter, she thinks Matthew caused this somehow. That he willed it. It's not rational, but my daughter doesn't think rationally in moments like this."

Ava kept walking, and Deacon was right beside her. "You're looking for the cafeteria, I imagine," he said. "Mind if I come along with you?"

Ava just shrugged her shoulders and kept walking. Deacon apparently took that as Ava nonverbally suggesting that she wanted his company, and Ava was grateful for his presence.

She was also grateful Deacon had the presence of mind to negotiate the hospital maze. She couldn't read signs in her mindset and couldn't interpret them even if she could read them. But Deacon gently guided her down one hallway and then the next. Before Ava knew it, they were entering the cafeteria.

"Sit down," Deacon said. "I'll get you something to eat." He looked at his watch. "It's 7. You probably haven't eaten dinner, have you? Tell me what you like to eat, and I'll buy it."

"Anything," Ava said with a wave of her hand. "Whatever you bring me, I don't think I can eat it. I'm really not hungry."

"Well, I'll bring you something, and if you can't eat it, you can throw it in the bin."

Ava just nodded. She found a table and sat down. She looked out the window, and, just as Sarah had predicted, torrential rain was falling. How did she know it was going to rain? How did she immediately know Siobhan had meningitis? How did Ava miss it? She was going to take Siobhan into urgent care. She never even imagined she'd have to take her granddaughter into the ER. She never imagined the illness could be that serious.

But it was. Bacterial meningitis was something that could very well kill Siobhan. Or leave her with a permanent disability. Ava imagined how difficult life would be if her granddaughter was left with mental retardation or deafness. There would be special schools and medical procedures, and... she'd love her granddaughter just the same. But life for Charlotte would undoubtedly be more complicated.

Deacon reappeared with a trayful of food. "I didn't know what to get, so I just picked up a little of everything. Sorry." He smiled. "I have a sandwich, and a salad, and some hot food, too. Mashed potatoes and gravy and fried chicken. I mean, it looks kinda rank, the chicken, but it probably tastes-"

"Pretty rank," Ava said with a smile. She was going to try to be game. "It's hospital food. What do you want?"

Deacon laughed. "True, true. Maybe I should get a pizza for everyone, and we can eat it down here in the cafeteria. I can ask if they allow that."

"I think the cafeteria will close soon," Ava said. "I'll munch on that sandwich. You can't really screw that up too much, can you?"

Deacon sat across from her and started to dig into the chicken. "Well, it's not a five-star chicken, that's for sure," he said. "I can always use it as a frisbee."

"Quinn has a dog," Ava said. "She'll eat it for sure."

"Let me get a doggie bag," he said. "In the meantime, I'll eat this salad. It looks okay."

He got up, got a container, and then put the chicken and mashed potatoes into it. "For Quinn's dog, Kona," he said, raising the container and nodding at Ava.

"She'll love it. She's the sweetest pup in the world."

Kona was some kind of a pug-shepherd mix that Quinn had found in a Manhattan shelter. She was a bit hyper, loved to play, was very protective and only barked when she heard something amiss. After living with Quinn in her tiny condo back in Manhattan for the first year of her life, she loved Quinn's new backyard.

Ava finished half of the sandwich and wrapped the other half up. Deacon finished his chef's salad.

"Thanks for this," Ava said. "I really need to find some food to take upstairs to the others. This sandwich was okay. Maybe I'll just get six of the same thing and call it good."

"Already thought of that," Deacon said, holding up a large white bag. "Sandwiches and cold chips for everyone." Then he showed her some cookies he'd also picked up. "And some biscuits."

Ava smiled. "You've thought of everything," she said.

"I did." He put his hand on hers. "You want to go back up, or do you want to hang out here more?"

Ava took a deep breath. "I want to go upstairs. They're probably wondering where we are right now. But I'm having a hard time keeping everyone together and not at everyone's throats."

But then she started to cry. Even though Hallie was taking her chemo well, Ava still was scared of losing her. And she really was terrified of losing her granddaughter.

"I'm so sorry, but it's just a lot. My best friend is battling breast cancer, and now Siobhan is critically ill. I'm afraid of losing them both."

"Don't forget, I know how you feel, especially about Hallie. My sister, she's doing great. And Hallie will be too. They caught it early. That's the important thing."

"Hallie will be fine," Ava said. "I know that. She looks great, actually. And Charlotte..." Ava shook her head.

"Don't get me started on that. She's so angry with Matthew that if something happens to Siobhan, she'll think he caused it to happen somehow. Thank God Jackson seems to be doing okay. I worry about him trying to make his way in the Hollywood world, but he has the temperament to make it through. And thank God Quinn seems to be doing well in her life. So, blessings."

"Everything will work out in the end," Deacon said. "You know what they say - when you're going through hell, keep going. No matter what happens, you can get through it."

"Thanks." She got her purse together and brought out a wallet full of money. "I owe you for these sandwiches," she said.

Deacon waved it off. "No worries, you can get me next time. I buy you a stale sandwich that has been in that fridge for days and days, and you can buy me a five-star meal at a five-star restaurant. How's that? That seems pretty fair if you ask me."

Ava smiled at his little joke and then leaned her head on his shoulder.

They headed back up to the ER, where Quinn, Hallie, Charlotte and Matthew were there.

Charlotte came over to Ava, tears in her eyes. "They're going to admit her," she said. "The doctor came out and told me she might not make it. She has a severe case, mom. Very virulent, the doctor said."

Ava felt the floor swallow her whole. This wasn't happening. This couldn't be happening.

"When are they going to admit her?" Ava asked.

"Soon. When they get a bed. The doctors are working on her right now. They're giving her an IV and antibiotics and doing all they can."

Matthew came over to Ava and put his hand on her shoulder. "Charlotte is exaggerating this a little bit. The doctor didn't actually say that he didn't think that Siobhan would make it. Charlotte only hears that because she's so scared."

"What *did* the doctor say?" Ava asked.

"He did say that Siobhan's case is serious," he said. "And virulent. But he also said that we probably brought her in on time. And she's being admitted. That part is true."

Ava calmed down a little when Matthew told her they probably brought Siobhan in on time, although the word *probably* sounded ominous. But she was still uneasy because Matthew also said that Siobhan's case was virulent.

She went over to Hallie and Quinn, who were sitting together.

"How is she?" Quinn asked.

"They're admitting her," Ava said. "And she apparently has a bad case. But that's all I know."

"She's in the best hands," Hallie said.

"I know," Ava said, wringing her hands.

Three hours later, and everyone was still in the ER. Siobhan was yet to be admitted, and the doctor came out and kept everyone informed from time to time. It seemed like the little girl had stabilized, which was a good thing and a bad thing. It was good because at least she wasn't getting worse. But it was also bad because it meant that she wasn't getting better, either.

"Please, Deacon, Hallie, Quinn, go home," Ava said to her friends and family. "There's nothing that can be done right now."

Everybody protested that they wanted to stay until they heard something more about Siobhan.

As if on cue, the doctor came into the waiting room. "I'd like to speak to the parents of Siobhan Killeen," he solemnly said.

Ava looked over at Charlotte, who was obviously terrified. She was sitting by herself in the corner, trying to put as much distance between herself and Matthew as possible. Since Matthew was sitting in the middle of everyone else, Charlotte had to separate herself from the entire group. Ava had been sitting next to her for the significant duration of the evening. Still, she felt that she had to hang out with everyone else as well, so she found herself going from her daughter to the group and then back again.

Matthew and Deacon appeared to be making friends. They were sitting next to one another and had been talking for the past few hours about guy things like football, *Marvel* and *Star Wars* movies, and *Minecraft*. They also found they both loved to surf, and they agreed to go surfing together within the next few days.

Charlotte watched Deacon and Matthew bro out together with evident disgust on her face when the doctor called the two of them to go back and speak with him. Then, when the doctor came out with such a serious look on his face, she caught Ava's eyes and shook her head.

"Can I bring my mom back, too?" she asked the doctor.

"Yes," the doctor said. "I'd like to speak with the three of you about Siobhan."

At that, the three of them followed the doctor to the ER room, where Siobhan evidently was.

Chapter Thirty

Charlotte

Ava followed the doctor back to where Siobhan was lying on a bed, hooked up to an IV. She looked so tiny and help-less in that bed that Ava felt like she would lose her breath.

Keep it together, keep it together, keep it together.

"I'm very sorry, but we're going to have to air-lift Siobhan to Boston. She needs to be in the ICU," Dr. Wagner said. "She was stable, but now her brain is starting to swell. I'd like to transfer her to the Boston Children's Hospital as soon as possible. When we get her to that hospi-tal, I'll need to put her into a medically-induced coma."

Ava felt her heart stop. She grabbed Charlotte's hand, which Charlotte squeezed hard.

She looked over at Matthew, whose eyes got huge when the doctor said that little Siobhan would be put into a medically-induced coma. However, he nodded his head and started asking questions.

"I understand," Matthew said. "You have to put her into

a coma because her brain is swelling. What is the process? How long will it take? How long will she have to be under?"

"We'll give her a dosage of Thiopental, which is a barbiturate. This'll reduce her brain tissue's metabolic rate and restrict the blood flow in her brain. This, in turn, will narrow the blood vessels in her brain and reduce the pressure on her cranium. We must act soon. If we delay, then there's a good chance that she'll suffer irreparable brain damage. She'll most likely lose respiratory drive during this induced coma, she'll have to be placed on a ventilator."

Charlotte just stared at the doctor, seemingly unable to speak. Ava opened her mouth to ask some questions, but Matthew spoke up once more. "How long will she be in this coma?"

"I don't know. Nobody can tell that at this point. It could be hours. It could be days. In some rare cases, patients are in a medically-induced coma for weeks, even months. Of course, we'll be closely monitoring her vital signs in the ICU. There'll be a doctor monitoring her EEG, blood pressure, and heart rate."

"And what are the side effects?" Matthew asked.

"The barbiturate can lower the blood pressure to critical levels, which sometimes leads to heart failure and impaired circulation. She could be susceptible to blood clots and infections, especially lung infections and pneumonia. She may have impaired gastrointestinal motility, which could cause severe constipation."

"And if we don't do this?" Matthew asked.

"If we don't do this, she could die very quickly. Her brain is rapidly swelling. If she survives, she could have profound irreversible brain damage. I'm afraid that this is a last-resort procedure because of all the risks associated with it."

Charlotte was gripping Ava's hand while shaking her head over and over and over.

"Do it now," she said. "Don't delay."

"Yes," Matthew said. "I agree. Please put her into a coma as soon as you can."

The doctor nodded his head. "She'll be air-lifted as soon as possible. I've already notified the transport, which will be here within minutes. You're doing the right thing."

"When can we see her?" Matthew anxiously asked.

"You and Charlotte can go on the air transport with your daughter. I'll help all of you onto the helicopter."

As the trio followed the doctor to the helipad, Charlotte leaned on Ava while sobbing. "She's going to die, I know it," she said. "Or she's going to have profound brain damage. What if she ends up deaf and blind? Historians think that's what happened to Helen Keller - she had meningitis and ended up deaf and blind. What then?" Charlotte gripped her abdomen and bent over. "My baby might end up deaf and blind or profoundly incapacitated. I want her to live her best life, but what if she ends up with profound disabilities?"

"If she ends up with profound disabilities, we'll deal with it," Matthew said. "It won't be the end of the world. We're both working. We can hire a nurse who can help us adjust. At least she'll be alive."

Ava listened to her son-in-law, thinking a body snatcher must've taken over. This guy never wanted his daughter at all, yet here he was, trying to reassure Charlotte that he'd be okay with that daughter living her life deaf and blind. Well, not okay with it, of course, but they would deal with it together.

The three of them made it to the hospital's roof, where a helicopter had just arrived. Dr. Wagner helped Charlotte and Matthew onto the chopper, and little Siobhan was also loaded onto it.

"Mom, I want you to come with us," Charlotte said, holding out her arms. "I need my mom."

Ava looked at Dr. Wagner, who shook his head. "Unfortunately, there's only room for two passengers. Ms. Flynn, you'll have to arrange your own transportation to the hospital."

"I understand," Ava said. "Charlotte, you can be strong. I love you." Then she whispered in her ear. "Let Matthew be there for you. He loves you and Siobhan very much."

Charlotte embraced Ava, boarded the helicopter, and then the chopper took off.

After the helicopter took off, Ava went back to the ER waiting room, where Hallie, Deacon, Quinn, and Jackson were still sitting.

"You guys might as well go home," she said, looking at the clock. "It's 2 in the morning. Siobhan is being air-lifted to Boston Children's Hospital, where she'll be put into the ICU."

Deacon came over to Ava and put his arm around her. "Air-lifted to Boston? ICU? Mate, that sounds serious. What's going on?"

Ava explained to the group about the induced coma. "There's not much that can be done, except wait. Matthew and Charlotte are heading to Boston with their daughter. So, there's nothing that can be done here anymore. Please go on home and get some rest, everybody."

"What are you going to do, Ava?" Quinn asked.

"I don't know," Ava said. "I'd like to go to Boston tomorrow. However, I'd almost prefer not to be there. I feel Charlotte and Matthew might be better off handling this on their own, together. After all, they're the parents. They're the ones who need to make all the decisions, not me."

Ava also secretly thought it'd be better for their marriage if she let them handle this crisis on their own. She was shocked and pleasantly surprised at how engaged Matthew had been about this entire illness. He had never even looked at Siobhan before. He threatened to divorce Charlotte just because Siobhan happened without his "consent." But Ava had to admit that Matthew now seemed to genuinely care about the little girl. Maybe the prospect of losing her is what finally woke him up.

If that was the case, there was a chance for their marriage.

Chapter Thirty-One

Charlotte

After Siobhan, Charlotte and Matthew were air-lifted to Boston Children's Hospital, the tiny baby was immediately taken to the ICU. Charlotte and Matthew anxiously went to the ICU waiting room.

After a matter of hours, Dr. Wagner came to find them. "Your daughter is now in a medically-induced coma," he said. "And is on a respirator. You can go and visit her if you like. When she's in this coma, she'll have bursts of consciousness. We call it burst suppression, which means that there'll be periods where the brain is active, alternating with periods where the brain patterns are very quiet. So, what that means is that there'll be periods where your daughter will be aware that the two of you are by her bedside. She'll have glimpses of consciousness. It'll be helpful for her, comforting for her, to have her parents by her side while she's in her altered state of consciousness."

Charlotte felt nauseated. She'd been feeling that way

ever since little Siobhan had been in the hospital. However, she was vaguely aware that Matthew was gripping her hand, and that comforted her.

She didn't know when she finally decided to let him comfort her. She wanted nothing to do with him when she was in the ER waiting room. But now, maybe because it seemed all was lost with their daughter, she allowed him to take her hand. To put his arm around her. To put her head on his shoulder. Her daughter was in critical condition. She could die. There was a good chance of that happening. Intellectually, she knew this.

She profoundly resented her husband because he never wanted Siobhan and was such a jerk about it. Still, she had to admit he seemed to be coming around. So, when he nodded his head and led her down the hallway to the ICU, where their daughter lay on a respirator, she let him.

Siobhan was lying on a hospital bed, a tube down her throat and an IV in her arm. A machine next to her kept track of her vital signs, such as her blood pressure, pulse and oxygen levels. Charlotte sat in a chair next to her daughter, and Matthew sat next to her.

"She looks so small. So helpless," Matthew said, staring at Siobhan. Then he smiled. "She really does look like Ava, doesn't she?" He reached over and smoothed a lock of bright red hair off her forehead. "She doesn't look like either of us."

"No, she doesn't," Charlotte said. "That's genetics for you."

Matthew took a deep breath. "How did things go with that Conrad guy?"

Charlotte shrugged. "I got the job. But I don't know if I can do it now."

"Why not?"

"My daughter might need me too much. I'm sorry, but my mind is going there. She might be severely handicapped from this. I can't take hours away from her by doing this job. I mean, it's basically work from home, but it's going to demand a lot of hours from me."

Matthew put his arm around her. "Honey, I don't think that spending 24/7 worrying about Siobhan will be good for your mental health. Now, tell me about the job. Tell me about Conrad. Let me try to talk you down."

Matthew was generally good at talking her down. That was his greatest strength, Charlotte realized. She tended to spin in her head, and get twisted in her thoughts. Her brain always seemed to go to the worst possible scenario, right from the start of any crisis. Matthew always helped her see the forest for the trees.

"He's great," Charlotte said wistfully. "I mean, he's very talented, and I'm excited about the book that he hired me to ghostwrite. But I just can't take the time away from my daughter."

"Our daughter," Matthew said gently.

Charlotte looked at him. "I thought you didn't want her. And didn't want me because you wanted both of us gone from your life. I thought you wanted to live your life free - hang out with your friends, go to the bars and go surfing and to brunch and whatever it is you want to do, whenever you want to do it."

Matthew shook his head. "No. That's not what I want. I want you. And I want her. I realize that now." He shrugged his shoulders. "Actually, I think I've been coming to that realization for a while. I don't know. I've been coming home to our empty house for the past few months and just… standing and staring at Siobhan's empty room and…" He took a deep breath. "I don't know. I've been in my head about her for a while. I haven't said anything to you because I didn't want to get your hopes up. But, yeah, I've realized that I've been a jerk for the past few months and that I really do want our family. Now, this. It's all been crystallized, you know? My priorities have been all wrong."

Charlotte swallowed hard. "What about your desire to live your life like a single dude?"

Matthew chuckled. "It's not all it's cracked up to be. David and those guys, they drink a lot. I don't think I realized just how much they like to party like they're still in college. Don't get me wrong. I think I'd like to party once in a while myself. Emphasis on once in a while. But it's not the life I want. I want my life to mean something, you know? And I think that being a father to my daughter and a husband to you would actually accomplish that. If that means anything at all."

Charlotte nodded her head. "Well, I guess if we got back together, we could figure something out. I mean, I know you need your space. You love to surf, and I hate the beach. And you love to go hiking and all that, and I-"

"Hate the outdoors," Matthew said with a smile. "I know."

"Yes. But, you know, if you wanted to go surfing once a week, or even more than that, I'd be okay with that. You can see your friends that way, too. And if you want to go camping with the guys once or twice a year, that's okay, too. I don't want to go, of course, but I don't want you to have to give that up."

"Well, my bud Tom does have a cabin in the Adirondacks that I'd like to visit in a few months. Go snowboarding and skiing and things like that." He cocked his head. "You'd be okay with me going?"

"Of course," Charlotte said. "But it's a cabin? I mean, I

could go, too. Just don't expect me to join you snowboarding and all that. I'll hang out in the cabin and do my thing."

"Maybe you can hang out in the cabin and work on your ghostwriting project?" Matthew asked. "Char, you really need to do this. You'll love it. I know you will. When I first met you, I remember how you were so into those artists you were studying. How fascinated you were by them and what their lives were like. You really came alive when you talked about that stuff. Kinda like when I come alive when I'm cooking and creating new dishes. I miss that Charlotte. The interesting, intellectually vibrant, passionate Charlotte. You've been so grey lately, Char. I miss the colorful girl I fell in love with."

Charlotte studied her daughter, feeling completely lost. She wanted to do the ghostwriting project. She'd never wanted anything more in her life. But could she take the time away from her daughter? Especially if her daughter ended up having special needs?

"I'll think about it," she said. "I mean..." She trailed off. In the back of her mind was her greatest fear. She would lose her daughter. What then? She'd be free to do what she wanted with her life, but it would be so empty.

She didn't finish her thought. She just sat there, staring at her daughter, not really wanting to talk to Matthew anymore. Matthew seemed to sense the change in her, for he, too, got quiet. He kept holding her hand, however. That simple act was all she needed to know that he was there for her.

After all they'd been through, he was still there for her.

And that meant the whole world.

Chapter Thirty-Two

Hallie

Hallie decided it was time she got back to work. She had so many dark days when she just couldn't get out of bed, and she felt like puking all the time. She had learned how to make many different kinds of dishes and goodies with cannabis, which helped keep her appetite up. Her antinausea medication also worked to an extent, but she was still exhausted.

Yet, she also knew that she was going stir crazy just laying in bed all the time. She felt she was dying, one day at a time. And she always lived by the motto that if you're not living, you're just dying. So, even though she was exhausted and sick and didn't want to do anything, she also knew that she needed to.

She knew Quinn would never say anything to her, but she saw the look of pity in her eyes. Quinn was afraid of losing her, and there was just no way that she could talk to

Hallie about it. Hallie knew this was the case, even if they had talked around it all along. So many things were unsaid between her and her best friend, so many words that weren't spoken, but didn't really need to be.

She got word from Willow that an artist friend of hers, Conrad, who also apparently was going to employ Charlotte in some sort of position, was looking for a life coach. "He's a really good guy, but he's very insecure. Really, he does need someone to talk to him and tell him how great he is so he doesn't get too down on himself. I'm sure there are other things you can do to help him, but, mainly, he just needs a boost to his ego."

Hallie found out about the project, and she was happy to get back out there, if only because she wanted to stop worrying her friend. So, when she got the word that she would meet with this artist, Conrad, she immediately went to tell Sarah about it. She wanted Sarah to go with her, in case she had problems. She also wanted Sarah to drive because she wasn't quite ready to get behind the wheel. She still felt weak as a kitten.

Sarah was more than happy to go with her. "I'm so happy to hear you're going to be doing this. But I want you to take it easy. You can't just throw yourself into your business like you did before. I mean, eventually, you're going to be able to go full bore. But, for now, you should probably go part-time."

Hallie knew that she was probably right about that. "I know what you're saying. Maybe I should just go ahead and take on Conrad and stop with that. It sounds like he has a lot for me to do. And, who knows, maybe I can take on some of his artist colleagues in a few months."

Hallie was actually very excited about meeting this Conrad.

She found his studio and walked right in, as the door was open. There, sitting on a stool and working on a canvas, was apparently Conrad Maxwell. His graying hair was long and styled in a man bun, and he had a very handsome face. Strong nose and chin, bright blue eyes. He looked like somebody who would be a great deal of fun, and Hallie had high hopes for this meeting.

He barely looked up from his canvas when she walked in. He pointed to a chair, his eyes not leaving the canvas for even a second. "You must be Hallie. Sit on that chair. Sorry, but I'm trying to figure this damn painting out. I'm trying something new. It is just not working out." He shook his head and then put his hand to his nose and squinted. "Ah, the lot of you need to bugger off." And he took one look at Hallie and Sarah and then smiled. "Oh, how funny. I said that the lot of you need to bugger off, but there's only two of you. So, I guess I mean to say that the pair of you need to bugger off."

Hallie cocked her head. She got out of bed for this. She was so looking forward to meeting with this guy, and he was already giving her the brushoff. "I'm sorry, I don't know what you mean. We arranged this meeting."

Just then, Conrad cocked his head at Hallie. He narrowed his eyes. "Oh, I get it. You're not leaving because you got out of bed for this meeting. You're wearing a scarf, and you have no eyebrows or eyelashes, so I guess I can assume that you're going through chemo. Bugger off anyhow."

Hallie crossed her arms in front of her. She knew she was going to probably not get this job, at least not with this guy's attitude at the moment. But she was going to let him know how she felt about it. "Mr. Maxwell, I don't know what bug crawled up your rear this morning, but I can assure you, it has nothing to do with me. I just happen to be the one in front of you, so you're going to heap your verbal abuse upon me. I don't know why you're in such a mood now, but I can tell you that it is extremely rude to set up a meeting with somebody only to throw her out the second she walks into your studio. I am a professional. I expect to be treated as such."

She took a deep breath. She didn't like the way he was looking at her scarf. So she took it off and stuffed it into her purse. So there she was, her head completely bald, her eyelashes and eyebrows gone. She ordinarily felt very self-conscious walking around without either a wig or scarf, but because she could not stand the way he was looking at her scarf, she decided to go ahead and show him her chrome dome glory.

To her surprise, Conrad actually nodded his head and stood up. "Can I get you some tea? I have some good ones. Oolong tea, have you tried something like that before? It's Chinese, a green and black tea combination, sweet after-taste. I also have some chamomile if you're not feeling that adventuresome. I would offer you a shot of bourbon, but it's 1 o'clock in the afternoon, and I gave up day-drinking a long time ago. I found out that I can get pissed while I paint, but it doesn't always turn out that great."

Hallie said nothing but just nodded her head.

"Good, good. Well, I guess you're going to be staying, so I might as well get your feedback on the painting I'm working on. Like I said, I'm bloody trying something new because I was bored with what I was doing before. There is only so many 'fuck the man' Dadaist BS that I can do before I just want to take my knife to the canvas and completely rip through it. Besides, I haven't been in such a hateful mood these days, not that I'm chuffed or anything either, but I haven't woken up really pissed-off in quite a long time. So, I'm trying for something kind and gentle. And I'm finding I hate it because it's so bloody boring."

Hallie felt a bit more relaxed. It seemed that he would give her a chance, after all, so she was happy she did not come here for nothing. She walked over to the canvas and saw he was working on a painting that resembled a deserted city street that was brightly colored, with vibrant oranges and yellows and blues and greens, but on closer inspection, was actually underwater. The giveaway for that was that there was a manatee at the very end of this brightly lit street.

Hallie smiled. Something was very soothing about this painting, which surprised her because his paintings were usually angry, edgy, full of vim and vigor and protest. He was trying something new, but it didn't seem to be on brand, so she wondered how fans of this guy - and he apparently had a lot of a fans, if his social media was any indication - would take to this new style. She liked it because she liked a lot of bright colors and whimsy, and maybe his fans would like it too. But she doubted it.

Conrad came back over to her with the tea, and he offered one to Sarah, as well. "I'm sorry, I didn't get your name?"

"Sarah."

He nodded his head. "I gather you're Hallie's friend?"

"Yes."

He sat down with the tea, sipping it almost daintily, which was weird. "Teatime, that's a British thing. I needed a break, anyhow. So what did you think about the painting?"

"I actually love it," Hallie said. "My eyes are drawn to

the bright colors and the manatee. He reminds me of the stories they used to tell about the manatees and how sailors mistook them for mermaids."

Conrad nodded his head. "Yes, that's very true. But that wasn't really why I put the manatee in there. Truth is, I just like manatees. They are very endangered, you know. They get caught in fishing nets, algae kill them, boats kill them too. It just seems that the most gentle creatures on this earth are the ones that suffer the worst fate, don't you agree?"

Hallie nodded her head. "Yes, I do agree with that. Is that the reason why you included the manatee in your landscape? And I thought that you said you were doing more soothing paintings because you're in a better frame of mind than earlier."

"I am in a better frame of mind, but I also said I'm not chuffed. As you can see, the street may be bright, but it's also desolate and deserted. And there is the little manatee, alone. You could take from this what you will, but I definitely do not believe this will be a joyful picture."

Since Hallie had taken the time to review an entire portfolio of Conrad's work before she came to meet him, she generally knew what his paintings were all about. And, now that she looked at it differently, he was right – it was a desolate street, and there was an animal alone on the street – she saw the heartbreak in it. And she realized the painting probably was not that off-brand after all.

"I can see that. Why don't we talk about some ideas I have for some publicity that I can get for your book and for your new gallery? I've been working on this all night, and I wanted to get your input too."

So, for the next couple of hours, the two went over her plans for him.

Hallie realized by the end of it that his bark definitely was worse than his bite. He definitely was a guy who spoke his mind, in no uncertain terms, but she was used to that.

And she figured that she could probably get used to him, too.

Chapter Thirty-Three

Charlotte

Days went by, and Charlotte and Matthew never left their daughter's side. Charlotte, for her part, started working on her ghostwriting project. Matthew had finally talked her into keeping the project, and she spent her time researching the topic.

Ava visited on the second day, bringing everybody with her when she came to the hospital. And Grandma Colleen, who lived in Boston, visited quite a few times. But Charlotte and Matthew had practically moved into the private room where little Siobhan lay in her twilight state. They made sure that they touched her often, stroked her and talked to her in a low voice.

The doctors were constantly in and out of the room. Every morning, there was a meeting between five doctors who stood by Siobhan's bedside. They discussed her condition and what they planned on doing next. And then, they gave an update to the anxious parents.

On the third day, Dr. Wagner did another spinal tap and announced the baby tested negative for meningitis. "She no longer has the disease in her body," he said. "That's the good news. The bad news is, her vital signs and her EEG do not yet indicate that she's ready to be brought out of the coma. But we're going in the right direction."

Charlotte and Matthew grew closer than ever as they sat by their daughter's bed, day after day. They talked more than they ever had before, about everything, just like when they were falling in love. Charlotte was reminded of those heady days when they would talk until 4 in the morning about their childhood, politics, movies, music, their families, and just whatever came to mind.

Charlotte found Matthew's presence a great comfort to her. "You know, if it weren't for you being here, I think I probably would've fallen apart," she said.

Matthew nodded his head. "Ironic, huh? Siobhan is what tore us apart, and she's bringing us back together."

The doctors came in just then, and, as usual, the team came in to meet. "I'd like to ask for the opinion of all of you on whether or not it's time to bring little Siobhan out of her coma," Dr. Wagner asked the doctors who were assembled around the bed. He went over the markers with the team members. "I've looked at her EEG, and it's my opinion that the swelling in this little girl's brain has decreased to the magnitude that it would be safe to bring her back to consciousness," he said. "And I'd like the input from the team."

Everybody took a look at the vitals and the EEG and agreed with Dr. Wagner.

"Okay," Dr. Wagner said. "It's settled. We shall start bringing her back to consciousness immediately."

Charlotte couldn't believe what she was hearing.

"Really? You mean, we might have our Siobhan back today?"

"Yes," Dr. Wagner said.

"And are we going to know right away if there was any permanent damage?" Matthew asked.

"We'll be able to tell right away," Dr. Wagner said. "We'll also do a battery of tests when she's well enough to ensure there's no permanent damage done to her brain, eyesight or hearing."

"What tests can you do to ensure she doesn't have brain damage?" Matthew asked.

"Besides the EEG, we'll monitor her response to stimuli. We use what's called the Glasgow Coma Scale, which assesses her verbal and motor responses to stimuli, as well as how her eyes react."

Charlotte called her mother, who said that she would be at the hospital as soon as possible. "I'll bring everyone up if you don't mind."

"No, of course not," Charlotte said excitedly. She was a mixture of elation and fear and dread. What if Siobhan was brought out of her coma, but she didn't react to light or sound? What if they put her through a battery of tests to discover she was profoundly brain-damaged? How would she handle it?

Then, with shaking hands, she went back to her daughter's bed.

Dr. Wagner then began gradually decreasing the drugs that were pumping through little Siobhan's body. "While I decrease the drug levels in her bloodstream, I'll closely monitor her brain activity and vital signs," he told Charlotte and Matthew. "This process will take 1 to 2 hours. After the drugs are withdrawn, she'll gradually regain consciousness."

Charlotte and Matthew sat around Siobhan's bed, anxiously watching the tiny baby as she gradually came out of her induced coma and opened her eyes. As Charlotte looked into those green eyes, she knew.

She knew she had her baby back and she would be okay.

But would she and Matthew be okay? After all, they were tentatively going to get back together. Or at least, they were working on that. And, if that were the case, she was going to have to come clean with him about what she did with the birth control situation. She couldn't have that secret coming between them anymore. She didn't want to have any secrets between them. She had to go forward with him in an honest way.

She thought about the prospect about telling him about her greatest shame, and her blood ran cold. Would he forgive her? Could she forgive herself? She didn't know. What she did know was that was a talk they were going to have to have.

Chapter Thirty-Four

Sarah

Sarah put a bid on the house she had her eye on, and because she was able to pay cash for it, she won the bid. So, she went to see her new little home.

The Miacomet Beach neighborhood was a quieter neighborhood than most, and the houses were much more spread apart from one another than in the Siasconset neighborhood. Nantucket considered the neighborhood to be one of its best-kept secrets. The neighborhood boasted a pond with snapping turtles, ducks, geese, swans, and various wading birds. The pond was a mile and 1/2 long, and people often used it to kayak and canoe. Since it was December, the leaves were off the trees, and the weather was so cold she had to wear a heavy coat.

Coming from Monterey, California, she wasn't used to cold weather. She had traveled the world with her boyfriend, Nolan, but they usually tried to get out of the cold weather during the wintertime. They would either go to the Southern Hemisphere in December, where it was summertime or go to a warm island like Jamaica. The exception to that was the Christmases they spent in Prague, Czechoslovakia. Sarah loved Christmases in Prague. Nonetheless, she was looking forward to her first Christmas on Nantucket. Especially because she had a new home to welcome in the new year.

There was also a golf course in the neighborhood, which was deserted and covered in snow. It was an 18-hole course, and even though it was open year-round, on this day, nobody was out.

There were also a couple of places to eat and grab a beer. A farm nearby, called Bartlett's Farm, offered tours of the farm and also had a farm-to-table restaurant. And there was a place called Cisco Brewery also in the neighborhood.

Her new house was a small Cape Cod with natural wood shingles. It had a front porch, and she loved that about it. Inside the house, she was looking forward to completely renovating it. It was a house built in the 1800s, so she knew she was going to have to get the proper permits to do what she wanted to do with it, which was to modernize it. Some of the windows were original, which meant they had the wavy look of very old windows. She didn't want to replace them because she liked how the windows made her house look like the historical structure it was.

But the previous tenants had installed shag carpet in the living room, and that had to go. She already knew she was going to have to replace the hideous carpet. Also, she had to get rid of the light fixtures, which were dated. With black-and-white checked tile, a clawfoot tub, and gold leaf framed mirrors, the bathroom would also have to be updated. The kitchen had a refrigerator from the 70s, and the stove was from about the same era. The cabinets were scuffed.

She had an idea to modernize everything, open up the floor plan, and raise the ceilings if she could. She hoped she would be able to carry out the floor plan she had designed for this house, but it remained to be seen if she could get the proper permits for that. She knew she could probably get the permits to change the floors and do other cosmetic changes, but she didn't know if she could get the proper permits to knock out the walls and raise the ceilings.

No matter. While she had a vision for the house, and, as she was trained as an architect, she knew she could make it happen, if she couldn't accomplish her vision exactly, she was okay.

She was able to buy this house, free and clear. She had breathing room in her life, financially, and that feeling was amazing. She still was going to work for Ava when Ava needed her. And she probably was going to work as a bartender during Ava's off-season. She really enjoyed the jobs she was doing. She had to work, anyhow, because all the money she got from the sale of the coin went into buying this home.

She couldn't wait to move in. She was going to start her new life soon, and it was all due to the generosity of a woman she never even met until recently.

It was funny how life worked.

Chapter Thirty-Five

Hallie

Hallie found she enjoyed working with Conrad, to her ultimate surprise. After their rough introduction, the two of them became really good friends. Hallie was delighted that Conrad willingly told her everything on his mind, even if it made him look bad. That kind of candor was refreshing to her.

"Hallie, don't get me wrong, I'm very chuffed about this gallery opening. But what if nobody comes to the grand opening? What if the people who come to the grand opening look at my stuff and decide it's all rubbish? What if they think that it's all derivative bullshit?"

"Don't worry, Conrad. I'll make sure that your show makes a splash." She worked with Conrad in organizing his life, and she also managed to find a gallery for a big showing. She helped him find a public relations firm willing to work with him to publicize the showing. She knew Conrad had quite a following. If he did not have that following, he would not be confident enough to show his work. But Conrad still felt insecure about his own talent, which Hallie actually found charming about him. And that was why she was working for him, too. Sometimes, life coaches really needed to encourage their clients, which was what Hallie was trying to do.

"That didn't answer my question," Conrad said. "You can get some warm bodies to come to an opening of an envelope if there's going to be free champagne and hors d'oeuvres. And it better not be pigs in a blanket and warm buckets of slop. Of course, the party is going to be a smash. But what I'm saying is that what if the people who come to the party think I'm nothing but a hack?"

"Conrad. Let me again show you some of the write-ups you have gotten from national art critics about your work." Hallie always had to bring out the clippings that she had found online from various arts magazines and newspapers, including the *New York Times*, which reviewed a show he had in Manhattan a few years back. The reviewer for *The Times* gave Conrad's show a glowing review. It talked about how he managed to make Dadaism relevant to today's audience and how the messages in his art were more accessible than most modern artists.

Even Hallie had to admit that you could look at Conrad's work and really see what he is trying to say, which was refreshing when modern art was defined by Marcel Duchamp's toilet. That was what the critics meant by accessibility, and Hallie thought that that was important. That accessibility was what allowed Conrad to reach a larger audience than he would have if he would've been just another artist who painted and sculpted obscure figures that were wildly open to interpretation, but Hallie suspected were often just meant as a joke that was played upon the world.

And so, Hallie once more got out the newspaper clippings and printouts of what people around the nation were saying about his work, to which Conrad would protest that that was then, when he had a voice and passion for his work, but this was now, when he was a hack. And after he said that, Hallie would always volley back that his work was the same quality as back then and that he had actually grown as an artist over the years, so his paintings and sculptures were more mature now than they were then. And so it went.

One evening, on the Friday before Christmas, Hallie decided she would invite Conrad to a private party hosted by Sebastian Michel, the cannabis chef she had a wild crush on earlier, until she found out he had a supermodel-looking girlfriend, because, of course. She somehow knew a private party featuring cannabis-infused foods would be right up Conrad's alley, and Sebastian let her know she would be free to bring anybody she wanted. She thought about Quinn and Ava, who were game earlier to go to Hallie's first cannabis-infused dinner party, back when Hallie was trying out medical marijuana for the first time. This was several months ago, but it seemed like years. But she had the feeling Conrad would really enjoy a party like this.

Hallie was correct in her assumption because, when she invited him to this party, he clapped his hands with delight. "Oh, when I saw your bald head for the first time, and I knew you were undergoing chemo, I thought maybe you would be into the weed. And now I know you are, and I can't tell you how delighted I am about that. Yes, I would love to go to a party with cannabis food."

So the two of them headed over to Sebastian's palatial

home, which was in a million-dollar neighborhood right by the Historic District, where Sebastian had his cooking studio. When Hallie went to the beautiful home, she realized how much money there was in what Sebastian was doing, and she wondered if she missed her calling. Not that she was ever interested in cooking, but she had to admit there was green to be made by cooking with the green.

Conrad dressed up for the occasion, wearing a pair of slacks, a button-down and a tweed jacket with patches on the sleeve. He looked like a professor, even with his man-bun. Hallie found him very handsome that night.

Sebastian opened the door, and they found a party in full swing. Sebastian took one look at Conrad, raised an eyebrow, and looked over at Hallie. "This is your guest? Conrad Maxwell?"

"You've met," Hallie said to Sebastian." Well, I guess the two of you need no introduction."

"No. I guess you might say we don't need an introduction."

Conrad looked at Sebastian with a quizzical look in his eyes. "I'm sorry, mate, I don't think we've ever met."

Sebastian looked over at Hallie. "No, I have never met Conrad Maxwell, but I know of him. Let me take your coats."

He took both Hallie and Conrad's coats and came back and offered them both a glass of wine. "You should probably drink this wine because the food I'm going to be serving will be *au naturel*. I didn't make cannabis-infused food because not all the people here are into that kind of thing, and I wanted to make sure I pleased all of my guests, not just the tokers."

So Hallie and Conrad both took a glass of wine, and they both found a place to sit down and sip it. In the living room, which was enormous, with 30-foot ceilings, hard-wood floors, walls of windows and modern furniture galore, and a 25' Christmas tree in the corner, there were probably at least 50 people milling about with wine and hors d'oeu-vres on their ceramic plates. The house had a view of the ocean, and Hallie could see the lights of distant ships on the horizon.

"What was that all about?" Hallie asked Conrad, refer-ring to how Sebastian pretended he knew him when he really didn't.

"Who knows? Sometimes people just get a bug up their arse for no reason. Sebastian, being a pothead, you would think he would be more mellow. And I have to say I'm gutted he's not going to bring out the weed in his food. I was actually looking forward to that."

Hallie watched Sebastian sitting among his guests, and she noticed she did not see Angelina, his girlfriend, anywhere. Sebastian caught Hallie's eye, and he motioned her to join him in the kitchen. Hallie just shrugged her shoulders, drank the rest of her wine in her glass, and went into the kitchen. "What's going on?"

"Nothing. I just wanted to talk to you alone and see how you're doing. You haven't been coming to the studio for the past few weeks, so I was worried about you. And now, here you are, with Conrad Maxwell, so I guess you're doing fine."

His voice had a bit of a hard-edged tinge, almost a veiled hostility, and Hallie inwardly wondered what that was all about. "Yes, yes. Of course, I'm doing fine. It was a rough few weeks in there, but I've definitely turned a corner, and I've been feeling better than I have in a long time. And what about you? Where's Angelina tonight?"

"We broke up." And then he cocked his head at Hallie. "And I know I told you that you could bring anybody you wanted to to the party, but somehow I thought you would bring one of your girlfriends."

"Why does that matter? I thought about asking Ava, Quinn or Sarah, but they're really not into this kind of thing. I felt maybe Conrad would be, and he is."

"How do you know Conrad?"

"He's my client. And, I have to admit, he's become my friend, as well."

"Your friend. Are you sure he's not more than that to you?"

Hallie couldn't understand why he gave her the 3rd degree like this. "No, he's just my friend." But even as Hallie said that, she realized maybe she did have feelings for Conrad. She certainly was entertained by him, she was intellectually stimulated by him, and she was in awe of his talent. That said, while she might have had romantic feelings for Conrad that she did not really acknowledge, she doubted he felt the same way about her.

"Are you sure about that?" Sebastian asked.

"Yes. But I don't understand your attitude right now."

"Hallie. I've had a few glasses of wine before you got here, so *in vino veritas*. I was hoping you would show up with one of your girlfriends because I was going to tell you tonight that I would like to start seeing you on a more social basis. I admire you for your courage in fighting this awful cancer beast, and I'm very attracted to you."

Hallie opened her mouth and closed it, not knowing what to say. She had to admit that since she had met this guy, she had been dreaming about this very moment, but she never thought it was possible because of his girlfriend. Now, here he was, offering himself to her, and she didn't know what to do. Because until he said something, she didn't realize she had feelings for Conrad.

She didn't know what to say, so she said nothing. At least nothing about what he had just brought to her attention. "I really have to get back to Conrad. I brought him here. It would be very rude just to leave him at a party where he doesn't know anybody."

"Conrad will be fine. There are enough people here who know who he is, and are fans of his, that I'm sure he'll find people to talk to."

Hallie was surprised Sebastian knew people who were followers of Conrad, but maybe she shouldn't have been. After all, Sebastian did run with a rather sophisticated crowd, so they probably were aware of the hip, up-and-coming artists in the area. Nonetheless, she felt she wanted to go back and talk to her client.

She went back out to the vast living room. There she saw Sebastian was correct. Conrad obviously did not lack in social skills, as there were several people talking to him, including a couple of women who were busy telling him how much they admired his work. She figured Conrad would be soaking up the praise, but he didn't look entirely comfortable talking to these women.

She caught Conrad's eye, and he stood up. "This would be a good crowd to mingle in," he said to Hallie when he came over to her. "These people seem to be loaded, so if you're looking for people who can afford my work, look no further."

Hallie took a sip of her wine, wondering if Conrad returned her affections. So far, it seemed that he did not. He was talking to her like she was his life coach, which she was. He was talking business, and this was her job, anyway. She was supposed to be looking out for opportunities for her client, and an upper-crust party such as this one was a prime target. So she would have to look at the party with an eye toward inviting people to the gallery showing.

So, Hallie wandered around the party for the next half hour or so, making contacts and talking to people about Conrad. She was surprised about how many of them actually knew him and what he did. A few were even avid followers of his. She got the word out about his gallery showing, and, by the time dinner was served, she had quite a few people who were committed to coming.

Sebastian finally announced that dinner would be served, so everybody headed into the dining area. There was an enormous table that could seat up to 30 people in this dining room. On his back patio, there were several other tables. Hallie was excited about what he would serve for dinner, and, of course, he did not disappoint. The Cornish game hens with cornbread stuffing and green beans were simple yet elegant, and the game hens were cooked to browned perfection. For the vegetarians who were in attendance, they feasted on stuffed eggplant with a side of couscous, and they, too, raved about their meal. Hallie noticed Sebastian was looking at her and Conrad, and she had mixed emotions about his ardor.

However, by the end of the evening, Hallie was readier to say yes to Sebastian and his offer to take her out on a date. Conrad had given his phone number out to a sexy brunette who was poured into a low-cut nude-colored gown that showed off her runner's legs. Hallie had no idea if Conrad had made a date with this woman, but she could tell by their body language that they were flirting with one another. And then Hallie realized her relationship with Conrad was all in her head.

So, she went to find Sebastian, to ask him if he was still

interested in going out with her. However, she couldn't find him anywhere.

"Where did Sebastian go?" she asked Amber, who was with one of Sebastian's dinner guests.

"I heard he went out to get some more liquor. He'll be back."

He didn't come back in the next 10 minutes, however. By that time, Hallie had left with Conrad. Conrad told her he had a massive headache that just snuck up on him. So Hallie could not get her message to Sebastian that she was interested in him, too.

Chapter Thirty-Six

Charlotte

After the scare with her baby daughter, and after the days of bonding with Matthew, Charlotte was ready to work with Hallie on how she could go forward. She was finally ready to understand her rigid beliefs about motherhood and family, and she was also ready to change her mindset.

Hallie was not feeling very well, because she had a few setbacks with her chemo. But, she was excited to be working with Charlotte, anyhow. "Okay, so you had a life-threatening emergency, and you've talked with your husband. So, are you ready to journal about an alternative life? A life where there is enough flexibility for the two of you to have a little bit of breathing room from one another once in a while?"

Charlotte nodded her head. "Yes. I'm finally starting to understand that I was a warden for Matthew. I've always had in my head that a mother needs to sacrifice everything for her child. And I've always had it in my head that a father needs to sacrifice just as much for the happiness of the child. And I'm starting to understand that it's not selfish to want to have a few things in my life that make me happy. Like hobbies, seeing friends, exercising, that sort of thing. And, it's important Matthew have the same thing in his life. So, I need you to help me with a life plan that includes outside interests. I still can't visualize it, but I want to. I really want to."

So, that's what Hallie did. She and Charlotte wrote out a plan. That was the best way for Charlotte to be able to integrate her new views on family life. She had to see it in writing.

And after she had it written out, it was time to share it with Matthew.

Chapter Thirty-Seven

Charlotte

Several weeks after Siobhan came home with Charlotte, back in the rooms they were taking up in Ava's house, Matthew asked Charlotte to move back. Even after Siobhan got better and they were no longer bonding by her bedside, Mathew and Charlotte continued to see one another. Charlotte was afraid that Matthew might change his mind again. Maybe it was just the fear of losing his daughter that made him break down the walls he had about having a family.

But, Matthew assured Charlotte that he was ready to be a real father and husband. She was going to have to keep her end of the bargain, of course, which was she was going to have to keep working for Conrad as a ghostwriter for his historical novels. She was really excited about that project, so she readily agreed to that condition. She knew why she wanted to do that. It was pretty simple, really. They needed a financial cushion. Matthew got another job, making what he was making before, around $60,000 a year. But that money proved to be barely enough to make ends meet for the family.

So, with Charlotte bringing in money as well, the stress of being financially strapped was going to be lessened. And that was important to both Charlotte and Matthew.

Another condition Matthew put on the situation was he needed to have some kind of down time. He wanted to be able to surf, sail, and go to the beach with the guys during the summertime. He wanted to be able to do that at least once a week. And, in the wintertime, he wanted to have a beer with the guys at least once every couple of weeks. Just as importantly, he wanted Charlotte to have the same down-time with her friends. He wanted her to get in touch with some of the friends she had lost contact with since the birth of Siobhan.

"It's important we have something just for ourselves," he said. "Otherwise, we're both going to feel suffocated. And I also want to go out on a date with you at least once a week. So, we'll have to find dependable help - somebody who can watch Siobhan during those evenings. I'll be happy to watch Siobhan while you see your girlfriends, however. And, no, I don't consider to be babysitting. She is my daughter, after all."

Charlotte was happy to meet all these conditions because she thought they would be good ones. Matthew was right. She was so focused only on Siobhan before, and she became a ball and chain for Matthew, because she didn't want him to see his friends at all. She expected too much of him because she wanted him to only spend time at work and at home. She had to let go of the beliefs that both of them had to be a family 24/7, to the exclusion of outside interests. She knew that by letting go of that belief, they would have a much healthier relationship.

Hallie had helped Charlotte with overcoming her thoughts about marriage and family. She was very happy for Hallie's guidance on that.

Now, she had to tell Mathew her big secret. And she was terrified about that.

"Okay, Matthew, I have something to tell you." She took a deep breath. "I lied to you. I told you I was on the pill, and I really wasn't. I didn't want to trick you at all. That wasn't the reason why I stopped taking the pill. I stopped because it gave me migraine headaches and mood swings. I also couldn't sleep very well because of the pill. My doctors tried to put me on different kinds of pills, but none of the pills were better than any other ones. So I just took myself off of them and started going with the rhythm method. I carefully tracked my cycles each month, and I wouldn't make love with you if I thought I was ovulating. Apparently, I messed up, which is why I got pregnant. I am very sorry."

Matthew nodded his head. "You know, if you would've told me this a year ago, I would've been furious with you. It took me such a long time to get to where I accepted my role in this family. It took even a longer time for me to embrace it. And now, when I look at our beautiful daughter, I couldn't imagine life without her. So, you're going to be shocked when I tell you this. But I'm happy you did that. Because if you had taken the pill like you were supposed to, you wouldn't have gotten pregnant. And we never would have become a family because I never wanted it. But it was forced on me by your actions. And, as I said, if you had told me a year ago, I would have hit the roof. But I'm really happy now."

And that was it. Her secret was out. And Matthew reacted how she always dreamed he would.

He loved her, and he loved their daughter.

And that was all that mattered to both her and Matthew.

Chapter Thirty-Eight

Ava

It was December 20, and Ava had Christmas Eve on her mind. She was getting the house ready for the intimate gathering that she would have for her friends and family. She didn't open the inn up to anybody else for Christmas Eve because she wanted it to be special for the people she cared about.

Jackson came over to help her with the decorations. Ava got a 10-foot tree that was to be trimmed with ornaments that she collected since she was a little girl, along with several that she had accumulated during her marriage to Daniel. Included in the ornaments were some that her mother bought for her and her sister, and those always made her feel sad because of all the wasted years she and Sarah didn't speak. They were good now, though, so the ornaments also made her happy.

Her heart always broke a little when she looked at the ornament she and Daniel bought during their first year of marriage. It was a small version of a 1929 Rolls-Royce because that was the car they had rented for their wedding. It was very difficult to find a person who would be able to rent this vehicle out to them, even in New York City, which was where they got married, but Ava said it was important to her that this was the car they would drive off in from the church and from the reception.

"I've always dreamed about this car," Ava told Daniel. "My grandfather wanted an automobile like this. It was all he ever wanted. He died not having the money to buy something like this or even rent it, and I promised him on his deathbed that I would do my best to fulfill his dream of riding in a 1929 Rolls-Royce."

So Daniel moved heaven and earth to make his new wife's dream come true, and he found somebody that could rent them a cream-colored 1929 Rolls-Royce. Ava had to admit it was probably the most unusual vehicle anybody could rent for their wedding. She got lots of comments about it when the two of them drove the car to the airport, where they got a flight to Barbados for their honeymoon.

She got to the ornament and just stared at it. Jackson came over to her and put his arm around her. He understood what she felt when she looked at this little car that she would hang on the tree. He knew that whenever Ava looked at the car, she thought about his father, the only man she ever truly loved. She loved Deacon, too, but not like she loved Daniel.

Ava wasn't going to be melancholy. She always had to keep a smile on her face during the Christmas holidays. That was always her mandate for any holiday season – she never let her children see her depressed or sad, especially when they were supposed to be happy, as everybody was supposed to be for Christmas. Christmas wasn't supposed to be a time for sadness.

With a great lump in her throat, she put the car ornament on the tree. Then she told the story to Jackson, the same story she told him every year. By now, he had memorized it. "Your father and I, from the first year we got married, decided we would get a special ornament we can use as a keepsake from year to year. The first year we were married, he wanted to get a special ornament he knew would always make me smile. So he got me a tiny replica of the car that ushered us out of the church after our wedding."

She was happy Jackson didn't try to tell her not to tell the story again or that he was over hearing about it. He simply smiled and pretended he had never heard her tell him about the ornament before. He always let her show her sadness over not being with Daniel over the holidays, and not having had Daniel all these years to watch Charlotte, Jackson and Samantha grow up into the upstanding adults they were. Yes, they all had their issues. Charlotte tended to be just a little bit controlling and slightly neurotic. Jackson was the opposite, but he was a little bit too free-spirited, and Ava worried that he didn't take life seriously. Samantha, up until recently, was a flighty mess.

But still, Ava didn't have any significant problems with any of her children, and she had to think Daniel was proud of them, wherever he was. And, for some reason, it was always around Christmas that she thought about the children's father this way.

Ava took a deep breath when she saw all the other ornaments she would put on the tree. The first ones to put on the tree were the three baby bootie ornaments Daniel bought when he first found out Ava was pregnant. He bought three identical baby bootie ornaments because there would be three children coming, and all of the ornaments were made of real silver. He never got the chance to put these ornaments on any tree, as he was killed several months before Christmas in the year the children were born.

Next were the ornaments Ava had bought for the dogs she had with Daniel, a cocker spaniel named Lucy and a pug named Velma. They both were puppies when Daniel was killed. Ava had doted on these dogs as if they were her children, and she bought each of them an ornament that looked just like them. Both dogs died of old age, one at the age of 15, the other at the age of 16.

"How come you don't have dogs right now?" Jackson asked Ava as he hung the two dog ornaments on the tree. "I remembered how much you loved those dogs. Now you have a big house with a large yard." He was referring to the front yard of the house, which was bounded by a white picket fence, as the house didn't have a back yard, only the huge deck. "And a beach to run on. And think about all those homeless animals who would just love to have a dog mom like you."

Ava nodded her head, thinking he was right. It had been a few years since she had a dog, mainly because when Lucy and Velma died, she grieved both of them immensely. But her life had been so crazy busy, working so many hours at the law firm, and she no longer felt that she had the time to spend with a dog. Her children were teenagers when the dogs had passed away, and she was having trouble with Charlotte's rebellion. She just didn't feel she had the mental energy to devote to furry children.

But Jackson was right – Ava was definitely in a different space now than she had been in a while, literally and figuratively. She now had a nice yard for the dogs to run in. She was going to get more than one dog if she were going to get any, because that was the way she did it – she always felt dogs needed a companion dog to keep each other company. And she was literally home all the time, even if she was constantly busy doing something while she was at her home.

She worried a little bit that her bed-and-breakfast would have to have a limited clientele if she got dogs, because she would no longer be able to take anybody who was allergic to dogs or didn't like them. But, considering she was full up all the time during her busy season, with a long waiting list, she knew she could afford to be a little bit selective. And, truth be told, she also knew that having dogs on the premises would actually be a great draw for many people. She would revise her website if she decided to go ahead and adopt some furry babies, because she would put pictures of her dogs on there so that everybody would know what to expect if they rented a room.

Of course, Sarah was staying with her, and Sarah had her beautiful pit bull mix, Bella. But Sarah soon would be moving to her own place, and taking her dog with her.

Ava also was thinking about getting some dogs because they were always a great company for her. There was nothing like a dog giving her puppy kisses that could compare.

"Maybe after the holidays, I'll think about adopting some shelter animals," Ava told her son.

"I hope you do," Jackson said.

"I will," Ava said wistfully. She was lost in thought about how she and Daniel had adopted Lucy and Velma from the Humane Society in New York City. They were brought in together, as they apparently were wandering the streets. They were both six months old, or around that age, and they were in the same enclosure. Daniel was the one who convinced Ava to adopt them, even though Ava didn't really want to, because she was so busy in law school, and she soon would be busy with three children as well. But Daniel was a freelance photographer, and he did a lot of his work from home, editing the photographs he took. He told Ava he would have the time to look after the puppies, so she agreed with him. And, she had to admit, she fell deeply in love with them from the second they came home.

Ava sighed. She always loved trimming her tree, and she really loved the fact that Jackson was with her this year to help her because she always had the kids help her put ornaments on the tree and all the trimmings. She always made eggnog for the kids – Charlotte, Samantha and Jackson really loved her homemade eggnog – and she always played Christmas carols while she and the kids brought out the ornaments and the angel that went on top. But every year it was the same – the ornaments always made her feel a little bit sad for the life that she had with Daniel, and the life she missed with him all these years.

Jackson understood her melancholy. He was always much more attuned with her than Charlotte was. And he knew that what she really needed from him was distraction. He gave her the space to grieve the life she didn't have, but he also knew when to jump in with either a joke or an optimistic tale about his life.

"So, I was about to tell you about my great news on the phone when I called you from LA."

"Oh, yes," Ava said. "I'm so sorry I haven't asked you about it. What's the great news?" Ava carefully brought out some other ornaments, the standard ones that didn't have meaning for her, but were pretty nonetheless. The Santa Claus, the Rudolph, the Christmas tree, the candy cane, the sleigh filled with toys, all of them solid gold, all of them given to her by her mother over the years. And all the round balls, red gold and silver, that filled out the tree.

"I got a named speaking role," Jackson said as he dug into the box that held the string of lights that went around the tree. "In a Netflix original series. It's a 1940s murder mystery, a miniseries that's based on a hit book. I have a small part in the third episode. Ironically, my character is a photographer. Just like dad."

Ava clapped her hands, and wrapped her arms around Jackson. "That's wonderful news! That's probably the greatest Christmas gift you can give me!"

Jackson just nodded as he strung the lights around the tree, and plugged them in. "How did Charlotte and Samantha get out of doing this, by the way?" Jackson asked, referring to the tree trimming.

"I just gave Charlotte a pass this year, because she's been through so much in the past few months. Samantha's busy making a cake for a big holiday party. Besides, I wanted to spend some quality time with you to see how you're doing. It sounds like things are going very well, so it will be a very merry Christmas indeed."

"Yeah, Charlotte certainly has been through a lot. She almost lost both her marriage and her child. It will be good to see her on Christmas Eve because I haven't talked to her too much for the past few weeks."

That was very unusual, as Charlotte and Jackson tended to be very close.

"Well, I'm sure she'll be happy to see you."

"Is gran going to be here on Christmas Eve?"

"She is." Ava smiled as she realized how happy she was about that fact. She and her mother were good, really good. They hadn't been for many years, but that all recently changed, and they had gotten close.

Ava unpacked another box of ornaments and smiled when she saw what was in this box. There was an ornament that was a sterling silver baseball bat and glove, and an ornament that was a sterling silver football helmet and football. Those were the ornaments she bought for Jackson, for her son was proficient in both these things. And then she brought out an ornament for Samantha – a sterling silver representation of a pair of ballerina shoes that Ava bought for Samantha during the phase when Samantha thought she would be a prima ballerina on the New York stage. That didn't last long, however, as Samantha didn't like all the hard work that went into trying to attain that particular dream. But Ava took her to lessons for several years, anyhow. And then there was an ornament that was a pair of pom-poms, as Charlotte was a cheerleader for a hot minute, but she gave that up too because she got into a fight with the head cheerleader on the squad and quit in a great blaze of glory.

Jackson took a look at the ballerina ornament. "I can't believe you still have this. Where did you find it?"

"In this box. I've always had it, it's just that you haven't been around for the past two Christmases to see it."

"And these pom-poms?" Jackson shook his head. "You're going to be opening up a can of worms."

Jackson referred to the fact that Charlotte got suspended from school when she and the head cheerleader, whose name was Jana, got into a girl fight, complete with hair pulling and kicking. That was when Charlotte quit the squad, amidst rumors going around that Charlotte had slept with Jana's boyfriend. At the time, Charlotte was a virgin, so this particular rumor was particularly insulting to her.

Ava hung the pom-poms up on the tree. "Come on, that

was so long ago. I can't imagine she'll be too insulted to see this ornament."

"You don't know Charlotte. I'd leave it off the tree."

Ava reluctantly put the ornament back into the box. She liked to hang up every ornament that she had. That was just one of her things. It was almost superstitious for her. She felt if she didn't hang up every ornament, somehow, bad luck would follow. So, when Jackson got up to get a glass of wine for himself and a gin and soda for her, she secretly took the pom-pom ornament back out of the box and put it on the back of the tree where nobody was probably going to see it, as the tree was facing a window.

Jackson came back out. "You put that ornament on the backside of the tree, didn't you?" he asked with a smile. "You're playing with fire, mom. Charlotte's going to sniff that one out."

Ava took the gin and soda in his hand, and took a sip. She could never pull a fast one on Jackson, it seemed.

Jackson got out a ladder and put the angel on top of the tree. Jackson got down off the ladder and took a sip of the wine, and the two of them stood back and admired the tree. It was beautiful. She bought it flocked, so it looked like the branches were snow-tipped. It was 10 feet tall, with white lights – Ava preferred the white lights, as opposed to multi-colors, because she thought it looked classier. She loved the ornaments on the tree, because they represented her life. Her life, and her family's life. And they represented Daniel, which was very important to her as well.

After Jackson left, Ava stared at the tree. She was completely alone in that she had closed down the inn just for the day so that she and Jackson could trim the tree together, and in that moment, she felt her aloneness. She felt all the emotions of the life that she never had with a man who she loved all these years. She felt sadness that she only had a few years with Daniel. He never got to see the football or baseball ornaments, nor the cheerleading or the ballerina ornaments. He would've appreciated them, as he was the one who had the idea about getting ornaments to mark the important points in both of their lives. Christopher never appreciated the ornaments, so she stopped buying them when she was with him. But Daniel, he would've been all about this tree.

She built a fire, sipped her gin, and wondered what life had in store for her in the coming year. Things were going very well with Deacon, but would they continue like that? She didn't know. She took it one day at a time. He was such a good guy, but she could never quite lose herself with him. She was too afraid of being hurt, so, even though they were together, she didn't allow herself to fall head over heels for him.

She still felt the sense that Daniel left a hole in her heart.

And, for some reason, it was always the holidays that made her miss him more.

Chapter Thirty-Nine

Ava

Christmas Eve was finally here, and Ava was very excited. She absolutely loved this holiday, and she always did.

Her mother, who apparently had nothing better to do during the day, announced to Ava over the phone that she was going to be coming over early to help her get things ready. It wasn't a question as to whether or not Ava wanted her there early. No, as was usual for her mother, it was a statement. She was coming over at noon, whether Ava liked it or not.

Truth be told, Ava was grateful for the help. She didn't have Reilly to cook for her, so it was up to Ava to bake the ham, make the sweet potatoes and mashed potatoes, make the green-bean casserole, bake the bread and make the pies, make the salad and supply the alcohol. On top of it all, she wanted to make cookies from scratch.

So, when her mother came over at noon that day, Ava handed her an apron. "Since you're going to be here, I'm going to put you to work in making the apple pie." Ava was terrible at making pie crusts. She could never get the right thickness, and usually, her pie crust ended up with holes in it that she had to patch up with other parts of the crust. She really should have just bought a crust from the grocery store. But, somehow, when she went to the store, she forgot about it. It didn't make its way to her grocery list. So she was left with the prospect of making the crust by hand, and since she hated doing it, she handed it off to her mother, who probably wasn't much better at making a crust, but it was what was.

"Dear," her mother said to her. "Do I look like Betty Crocker? Have you ever known me to make a crust by hand?"

Ava rolled her eyes. "No. But I suggest that today is the first crust that you're going to make. Think of it as the first crust of the rest of your life."

Her mother just shook her head. "I need a dirty martini if I'm going to be doing this. You got any olive juice?"

"What kind of question is that?" Ava asked. "Of course I have olive juice." Olives were Ava's favorite snack.

"Good." Then her mother went to Ava's pantry and got a bottle of vodka, a martini glass, and some olive juice. "I like my martinis very dirty," she said as she poured half the jar of olive juice into her glass. "Now, direct me to your flour, butter, and salt. But I'm warning you, your asking me to make a pie crust is like the blind leading the blind."

Ava got the ingredients out, and her mother put on an apron.

While her mother made the pie crust, and Ava handed her some apples to chop up, along with some walnuts, her mother drank the martini while she worked. In the meantime, Ava was making the cookies and glazing the ham.

"So, mom, how are things going with Barbara?" Her mother had recently met a new woman, and Ava was very excited her mother might get a second chance at love. She knew her mother had a hard time with the death of her longtime companion, Violet. And Ava also knew what it was like to lose someone you love like that. She hoped her mother could find happiness again.

Her mom smiled. "Things are going great, thanks for asking. No, I didn't invite her to this tonight. Things aren't going so well that we would spend the holidays together. But I like her. She's got spunk, she's very intelligent, and she challenges me. She's very different from Violet, who was so soft and such a girly girl. She's more like me, Barbara. But she's not quite as mean as I am."

Ava smiled. Up until recently, she wouldn't argue with her mother when her mother called herself "mean." But, she had gotten to know the real Colleen, and she knew her mother's sometimes acerbic demeanor masked a woman with a big heart. She was so happy she discovered that about her mother before it was too late.

"Mom, you're not mean. How is that piecrust coming along?"

Her mother shook her head. "I don't know why you suddenly think I'm the second coming of Rachel Ray." Ava looked at the piecrust and saw it was full of holes. Ava always had the same problem when she made piecrusts. They were always so difficult to roll out, so hard to get right. She wondered why it always looks so easy on the cooking shows.

Ava just smiled. "You're doing fine, mom."

Colleen raised an eyebrow. "Says you. Deacon going to be here?"

"He is."

"And how are things going with him?"

Ava grimaced slightly. "They're going fine. It's just that during this time of year I think about Daniel. Daniel was my Violet, you know. He was my soulmate. And I always get sad during this time of year that he never lived to see his three children thrive. It never seemed fair to me that he died before the kids were born. I don't know, whenever I trim the tree, I see the ornaments Daniel and I bought together, and it just rips my heart out every time."

"Well, you know what to do then," Colleen said. "You need to put those ornaments in a box and not bring them out. You can't really move on with your life until you put your feelings for Daniel in a box, as well."

"Is that what you do, mom? Were you able to put your feelings for Violet in a box?"

"Of course not. But I'm able to move on. When you get to be my age, you realize one thing. Life is too short to live in the past. Especially when you have something good in your present. You have a good thing, Ava. Don't ruin it because you can't get over the one who died."

Ava mashed the sweet potatoes, and added some butter, brown sugar, and cinnamon. She thought about her mother's words, and realized her mother had a point. There was no bringing Daniel back, as much as she always wanted to. Daniel was the past. Deacon was the present. She needed to realize that and truly open her heart to her handsome young boyfriend.

The snow that had been threatening started to come down. She hoped her guests would be able to get to her home without too much trouble.

This was going to be a great Christmas. Hallie was doing much better. She still had a few months to go in her chemo sessions, but she seemed past the worst of it. She was even working again, both at the spa and at her new business of helping people become the best they could be. Quinn was doing quite well with her daughter and with her business. Sarah was looking into buying a house of her own with the windfall she got from her rare coin. Her children were doing well. She and her mother were doing great.

She shouldn't be melancholy, but she always was.

Chapter Forty

Ava

6 o'clock, and everybody was starting to arrive. First was Quinn, with Emerson, who had her violin in its case. Quinn told Ava that Emerson would only go to the party if she could play for everybody. Ava readily agreed to that because Emerson was truly gifted with her instrument. Quinn said Emerson had a full repertoire of traditional Christmas music that she had memorized.

Also, Quinn was with a man. A very handsome man. And Ava knew that that man must be Asher. Quinn had confided to Ava that her heart was starting to thaw when it came to Asher, but she wasn't quite where she would be willing to let him in. Ava had never met Asher because Quinn didn't want to "parade" him around when she was unsure if he would last.

"It's like you don't introduce a new guy to your kid if you don't think the guy's going to last. I don't let my friends meet guys for the same reason," Quinn had said.

So, the fact that Quinn decided to bring him along seemed to be a good sign.

But, when Quinn talked to Ava in the kitchen alone, she played it off. "Asher, bless his heart, told me he had nothing to do tonight. I called shenanigans on that, but he's helped me find Emerson more times than I can count. So, I figured I might as well drag him along to this."

Hallie arrived with a bottle of wine in her hand, but she was alone. Ava was heartened to see Hallie, because her hair was growing back a little bit. It was short, but it was coming back in. And she gained about 10 pounds, which was good, because she'd lost about 20. Her eyebrows and eyelashes were coming back, as well. They were like fuzzy baby hair on her face, giving her the look of a soft baby chick. The color was coming back to her cheeks, and she seemed to have a lot more energy.

Ava cocked her head when she saw Hallie come in. "I thought you would be bringing either Sebastian or Conrad," Ava said, kissing Hallie's cheek. Hallie had explained to Ava that Sebastian was interested in her after all. However, she realized that she was more interested in Conrad. Maybe.

"Oh, I just threw up my hands. I had no idea which guy I wanted to invite, so I invited neither one. I'm sure that they both have plans of their own, anyhow."

"So, are you changing your mind about Sebastian?"

"I don't know. Conrad fascinates me because he is so blunt in his speaking, and he's so talented. But he's my client. And Sebastian, well, he fascinates me as well. Also because of his talent. But he seems a little posh for me. So I don't know. I just wanted to spend Christmas Eve with my chosen family, and not worry about either guy for right now."

Deacon was next. He came to the door and kissed Ava on the cheek. Ava could feel her face flushing. "Come in, come in. Let me take your jacket." She was shaking.

Deacon went into the gathering room, which was where everybody else was, around the fire. In the corner, Emerson was playing her violin. She was playing *Oh Holy Night*, Ava's all-time favorite Christmas standard. It was always a song that made her cry.

Next was Charlotte and Matthew, and Siobhan. They were such a beautiful little family now, Ava thought. She was so relieved that, for now at least, she didn't have to worry about her daughter. They came in the door, she took their coats, and they joined everybody in the gathering room around the fire.

Samantha and Grayson were next. Samantha was beaming. "Look what Grayson got me for Christmas!" she squealed. On her neck was a beautiful diamond necklace. Ava smiled. She knew soon there would be a diamond on her daughter's finger, too. Maybe not right now, but it was going to happen. Samantha and Grayson were made for each other.

Jessica and Andrew arrived. They were good friends, and had been for a while. But it was clear they were becoming something more. They were holding hands, and looking at each other with love in their eyes. Jessica was hesitant to get involved, of course, because you're not supposed to get involved during the first year of your sobriety. But they were each other's first love. They knew one another when they were five years old. It was obvious they were soulmates, and they were starting to realize it.

Sarah arrived. She was alone, but that was the way she wanted it. She was too busy getting herself together to have to think about a man in her life. She soon was going to be moving into a new home, and Ava was excited about helping her move.

Willow arrived. And Jackson arrived at around the same time. And Jackson looked at Willow, never having met her before. And if Ava wasn't mistaken, Jackson looked like he was knocked out by the beautiful psychic. His face flushed and he looked really shy as he introduced himself. Ava wondered if that was going to be a match. She hoped not. She liked Willow, but Jackson lived in Los Angeles. His ambition, from the time he was a young boy, was to be an actor. Ava wanted him to continue pursuing that dream, and she didn't want anything to get in his way. So, while she wanted her son to be happy, she also knew it would be complicated if he fell for somebody there on the island.

But it was obvious by the way he looked at Willow that he was very attracted to her. And Willow, for her part, had the same look in her eye.

As everybody gathered around to sing carols while Emerson played the violin, Ava smiled. She had the people around her she loved, and she was adding more people to the circle all the time. Last year, her mother wasn't really a part of her life. She didn't know Jessica. She didn't know Willow. Her kids were not around her last Christmas, for various reasons – Jackson lived across the country and Charlotte went to her husband's Christmas gathering. Only Samantha was around her last year. Now, all three of her triplets were with her.

And Sarah wasn't around her last year, either. Now, Sarah and she were so close. She could not imagine Christmas without her sister.

No doubt about it. She had expanded her circle this year, compared to last, and she was so happy about that.

She hoped she could keep expanding her circle for years to come.

vinci-books.com/beachfront-girls

When the past resurfaces, can love find a way to heal old wounds?

Ava's world is upended when her ex-husband Christopher resurfaces after a two-year absence. Despite her initial reluctance, Ava listens to his astonishing story that could change everything. Meanwhile, her friend Sarah runs for the school board with the help of seasoned campaign manager Max Stein, who harbors two secrets, one of which will shatter Sarah's world.

Turn the page for a free preview…

The Beachfront Girls: Chapter One

Sarah

Sarah had moved into her new home on Miacomet Beach and, having gotten the proper permits for all the renovations that she wanted, made her small home as shiny as the penny that had enabled her to buy this home in the first place. She was lucky that she got a compliant board who heard her permit requests because her home was built in the 1800s, therefore it was considered to be historic, and Nantucket was notorious for not allowing interior renovations in many of the historic homes.

But Sarah managed to get permits to do everything she wanted to do, which included raising the ceilings and knocking out walls so that the home, which had been decorated in early 1970s shag carpeting, combined with 1950s black-and-white checked tiles in the bathrooms, now was completely sleek and modern. It now had an open floor concept, with hardwood floors throughout, modern light fixtures, and a completely remodeled kitchen that featured an island, granite countertops, and even granite floor tiles in grainy black.

The ladies had helped, of course, and so did Deacon, whose job was contracting. Sarah paid all of them over their objections, and she paid Deacon's going rate, even though he, too, objected. But they were invaluable in getting her house together. They cheerfully brought over bottles of wine that they drank while they painted walls and helped her move in furniture she had just bought for the place.

When she left Monterey, she had very little to her name. Her dog, Bella, and souvenirs from around the world were all that she packed in her SUV because that's all she had in the world. She had been a longtime companion for a very wealthy man, and her life was reduced to whatever could fit into the trunk of her SUV. So, when she bought this house, she didn't have much of her own, but she had a ball shopping for couches, end tables, coffee tables, beds, light fixtures, bookshelves, desks, knickknacks, pictures, and just everything that was going to make her house a home.

Now, as she walked around her house with the cherry hardwood floors, the leather couches, the funky lamps, the flatscreen television, and a few vintage pieces - such as the real record player that she picked up at a thrift store that she filled with secondhand records that she bought at a vintage record store in Boston - Sarah felt an overwhelming sense of happiness.

This was her place. Perhaps for the first time in her life, she was living in a place that was only hers. It didn't belong to a billionaire who kept her in the manner he desired, and she wasn't sharing it with a roommate or her mother. This place was hers, and that meant the world to her.

Sarah was experiencing a bit of downtime in her schedule because it was still early spring. Ava, the sister who employed her, still had plenty of vacancies in her bed and breakfast, and her dining room was only about 25% full, so Ava did not want to have Sarah on full-time in her role as a sommelier. When Ava's business inevitably picked up after Memorial Day, and she once again had a full house and waiting lists, Sarah would return to working full-time for Ava as a sommelier and all-around utility help. Whether she was chopping vegetables, taking reservations, or helping to clean the rooms, Sarah was there for Ava for whatever she needed.

But, as it was only March, there wasn't a whole lot for Sarah to do. She was going to possibly try to find a job as a waitress in one of the restaurants, or a bartender position, but the sale of a very rare penny that was sent to her by Olivia, her deceased boyfriend Noland's wife, fetched almost $3 million and changed her life. Now she had money in the bank, a paid-for house, and getting a job during the off-season was no longer a requirement.

So, she was looking for something to do. And that something was looking after young Emerson, the daughter of her friend Quinn. Quinn was working 60 hours a week in her interior design business, and Emerson needed somebody to be there for her when she got home from school. So, that somebody was Sarah. She was delighted to watch the young girl because Emerson was wickedly intelligent, irreverent, and quite funny.

And so it was that Sarah found out about Emerson's new cause. Emerson was a very talented violinist, and she practiced the violin quite often. She didn't have to do a lot of homework or studying because she was just naturally a gifted student who got straight A's without even trying. And Emerson's mind was always moving at lightning speed.

Sarah sometimes had difficulty keeping up with her, but Emerson entertained her.

One day, Emerson came home and slammed down her backpack. "Dude," she said with a raise of her eyebrow. "You won't believe what my school is doing."

When Emerson came home, Sarah was sitting on the couch, reading a copy of *Architectural Digest*. She was an architect by training and constantly missed her old profession. She was considering renewing her architectural license, although that prospect seemed overwhelming. "What is your school doing?"

Emerson rolled her eyes and flopped down on the couch next to Sarah. "They're like talking about banning books, dude. We're talking things like *Huckleberry Finn, The Great Gatsby, Gone With the Wind, To Kill a Mockingbird, Catcher in the Rye, Beloved* and *1984.*"

Sarah narrowed her eyes at her young charge. "Oh my God. Sounds like the censorship police have descended upon Nantucket. It had to happen sooner or later, huh?"

"Yeah. I'm organizing a group at my school to protest this. It's some of the same kids I've gotten organized to petition the United States government to ban assault weapons and open more family planning clinics."

Emerson had managed to find, in her fairly liberal school, young progressives who were agitating for real change. The group put their words into action, and this action consisted of letter writing, petitions, organizing marches, and creating Tik Tok campaigns aimed at getting people to register to vote. Emerson also phone banked at the local Democratic headquarters once or twice a month. The teen was very interested in gun safety, family planning, climate change, and just about any issue that especially affected her generation.

And now, apparently, Emerson was also interested in censorship issues.

Sarah was amazed at the teen's energy, and the young girl inspired her. Sarah never really got into activism when she was young, although she knew her mother was active in causes.

"When is the next school board meeting?" Sarah asked. "I'd like to go and give them hell in person." Sarah had read almost all of the books that Emerson said would possibly be banned, and while all of them had disturbing elements, she didn't believe any of them should cease to be available to students who wanted to read them.

Emerson raised an eyebrow and smiled. "Aunt Sarah, I want you to go to that next school board meeting, which is next Thursday evening. But I think you should also run for school board. I think you would be perfect for it, and you don't have a whole lot going on right now. So you have the time for it."

Sarah smiled. "We'll see about that. In the meantime, though, I want to attend that school board meeting. You say it's next Thursday evening. At what time?"

"6 o'clock."

And so Sarah found herself going to the school board meeting of Emerson's school, which was called Thomas Jefferson Middle School. The issue of the book banning was one that apparently attracted a lot of people because the room was filled to capacity. The ten school board members were sitting at the front of the room, behind long tables, and most looked like they were girded for battle.

The school board members called the meeting to order,

reviewed some of the measures they proposed for the school, and then opened the floor for questions or comments.

One by one, concerned adults stood up to address their issues with the school. One parent complained that the school needed more after-school programs that were interesting to a wide variety of students because her young daughter was not interested in anything the school offered. Others had issues with other school policies. A few objected to the censorship issue, but there were others who were supportive. Sarah carefully listened to the arguments and made notes. She understood there were two sides, and she was determined to portray her side to the best of her ability.

Finally, it was time for her to speak to the school board. She stood up and cleared her throat. "I, for one, don't believe any books should be banned. Well, strike that. Obviously, books that are just sheerly pornographic and have no value to a young mind should be banned. But the books we're talking about are classics. And they deal with themes that our children will have to deal with sooner or later. They don't glamorize racism or suicide or murder - they're cautionary tales. For instance, *The Great Gatsby* is on the list to be banned because Gatsby and Daisy have an affair, but Gatsby ends up murdered, so how is that glamorizing extramarital sex? And for another instance, *1984* is a book that goes into the horrors of fascism. It doesn't glorify anything. And we need more books that deal with slavery and racism, not less. Everybody needs to be exposed to these realities of life, and the best way to expose our kids to things they might find repugnant is through art and literature. Young minds can be molded by art and literature, which is why Nazis were so anxious to ban anything that didn't hew to their ideology."

Then Sarah sat down, and a man stood up. He was a good-looking guy, dressed in khakis and a light blue button-down, his dark hair cut short on the sides and long on top, with large green eyes that were currently flashing anger in Sarah's direction.

"I'm so sorry, Ms. Flynn, but the moment you start talking about Nazis, you lose me," he said. "Banning these books is not the first step towards Nazism or fascism. It's simply protecting our young children from concepts they're not ready for. I don't want my 13-year-old daughter to have access to a book where a mother kills her child, a young boy drops an F-bomb every other word, or the N-word is used flagrantly. Many kids can handle these themes, but many can't."

Sarah made a face at the guy. And then she opened her mouth to defend herself, but this guy wasn't finished. "And, Miss Flynn, I understand you don't have a kid here at this school. I don't think you have a dog in this fight."

How dare he? Just because she was childless meant she didn't have a say in how young people were educated? Her childless status meant she couldn't care about the future of the nation's youth? Even if she didn't have young Emerson in her care five days a week for a couple of hours every day, she still would care about issues that affected young people. They were the future, and they were the ones who would have to live with bad decisions that adults made for them. And they didn't have a say.

Sarah stood up again. "I'm sorry, I didn't get your name," she said to the arrogant man who was still glowering at her.

"Max Stein," the guy said. "My daughter Julia is an 8th grader here at this school, and she read the book *Beloved*. She's been having nightmares about it ever since."

"Well, Mr. Stein, I resent you implying that just because I don't have a child, I don't have a say. I'm here to represent my young charge, who also is in the eighth grade and wants to have access to all the books that expand her mind. She understands, unlike you, that learning about scary ideas when you're young builds understanding of complex topics that will affect her life, and the lives of her peers, for generations to come. And, with all due respect, if an individual parent doesn't want their child reading a certain book, the answer is simple – that parent needs to tell the kid they can't have that book. The answer is not to say that no other kids can have access to it."

As Sarah sat down, half the room started to cheer for her, which was mixed in with a smattering of boos. She crossed her arms and glared at the guy. And while one person after another stood up and spoke, Sarah continued to glare at Mr. Stein. He just had such a smug look on his face, like he had all the answers for everybody. And if there was one thing that Sarah hated in life, it was a guy who thought he knew everything. Like this Max Stein apparently thought.

She wished she had at least one of her ladies there, if only because she wanted someone to rant to about the guy who dressed her down in front of everybody.

And after the meeting, Sarah knew one thing – she would run for school board. If only because she wanted to lord it over arrogant jerks like Max Stein.

The Beachfront Girls: Chapter Two

Ava

Ava was admiring her garden and the daffodils that were just starting to peek through the ground after having gone dormant since the previous summer when Sarah marched into Ava's house.

"Hey, girlie, what's going on?" Ava asked Sarah.

Sarah shook her head. "You won't believe the kind of arrogant jerk I met last night. You remember I went to Emerson's school last night to address the board about them banning some books, right?"

Ava nodded her head. Sarah had told Ava about her plans to run for the school board at Emerson's school, and Ava thought it was a pretty good idea. After all, nine months out of the year, Sarah didn't have much to do in her life. She worried about her sister. While Sarah never said as much, Ava thought that maybe her beautiful sister was a little bit lonely. Yes, Sarah had her friends there on Nantucket, and during the summer months, she was busy helping out there at the 'Sconset Inn. But, during the lean months, Sarah didn't have much going on, and Ava worried her sister would get bored.

So, her running for school board would be a good way to get active in the community and give her something constructive to do.

"Right, I remember," Ava said.

"Well, there was a guy there last night who had the nerve to imply that because I didn't have a kid in school, I didn't have a right to say anything about the school board's proposal to ban a bunch of classics."

Ava knew that the fact that she didn't have any children was a sore spot for her sister. It wasn't her decision not to have children. It was her ex-boyfriend Nolan's decision. Nolan lived to travel around the world for several months out of the year, so having children would, in his view, have been out of the question. While Ava understood the reasoning behind his decision that the two of them wouldn't have kids - it would be difficult to travel with children - Ava also knew that that decision broke Sarah's heart.

That was a regret Sarah carried around with her. Her sister wanted to leave the man 20 years ago or so because he did something unforgivable to her, but she didn't. She was railroaded into pleading guilty to a drug charge that she had nothing to do with. Nolan didn't help her fight the charge or the revocation of her architectural license. In fact, he wrote letters to the architectural board that damned her regarding the drug charge and lied and said she dealt drugs to children. He did these heinous acts because he wanted to control her. He knew that if she had a felony record and no architectural license, she would have no choice but to stay with him.

And so, even though she wanted to leave and find a life

of her own, she stayed. And that decision cost her her dream of having children of her own. So this guy standing up and dressing Sarah down by telling her she didn't have a say at the school board meeting because she didn't have children probably hit her where it hurt the most.

Ava put her hand on Sarah's shoulder. "Don't let it get to you, babe," she said. "You have a right to speak up. Emerson is a student of that school. Besides, the school board's decisions affects everybody in the community. If it affects our children, it affects us. So, you just speak your piece and don't worry about what others have to say."

Sarah just nodded her head. "I shouldn't let it bother me, but it does. It happened last night, and I'm still stewing about it. I don't know why I'm letting it get to me so much. Maybe it's because what he said was so hurtful or because he was so rude about it. I mean, who does he think he is? And he was just so smug about it. So arrogant."

Sarah shook her head.

"Hey, I know you're excited about getting involved with the school board. Just don't let that jerk get you down."

Ava never knew Sarah had any kind of doubt in her life. Her sister was always so confident. In high school, she was the queen, the beautiful girl everybody wanted to be around. Girls wanted to be her, and boys wanted to date her. Everybody just always flocked around her.

It was the same thing in college. In college, Sarah was a member of the Delta Gamma sorority, the best house on campus. There, as in high school, Sarah enjoyed immense popularity. Whenever Ava visited her on campus, she always had social events to go to. Parties, dances, gathering with friends – Sarah always had something going on because people always wanted her around.

But something happened along the way. Sarah lost her

special glow. Ava couldn't help but think that Nolan had much to do with that. He beat her down, probably because he recognized her special light that attracted so many people. The only way he could control her would be to extinguish that light. So, while Sarah seemed perfectly happy there on the island, there was also a kind of sadness about her. A regret that her life didn't quite turn out the way she had hoped it would.

And now, another man seemed to recognize Sarah's light and wanted to dim that light, at the very least. And Sarah needed some kind of moral support from her friends so she could pursue this school board position, which might go a long way toward giving Sarah back the confidence she always had when she was young.

Sarah said nothing but just looked around the garden. "It looks like the daffodils will be coming up pretty soon," she said. "Maybe if I don't get this school board thing, I can take up gardening. I've always wanted to learn more about it, but Nolan hired a team of gardeners to take care of our grounds. And, when I wanted to learn more about growing plants and flowers, he told me not to bother with it. But I just might bother with it now. After all, I have my own back-yard, and I'll need to plant some flowers to make it spec-tacular."

Ava furrowed her brows. There was definitely something going on with her sister. Sarah was just looking around the garden with a sad expression.

"What's going on?" Ava asked Sarah.

Sarah just shrugged her shoulders. "It's just hurtful. Sometimes I wonder what my role is in life. I guess it's just a hangover from feeling for so many years that I was useless. That's how Nolan made me feel. He made me believe I wasn't good for anything. And now I finally have latched onto something I hope will give me some kind of pride in my life, and this Max guy threw cold water on it. Now I feel like I shouldn't run for school board. Because he's right – I don't have a kid in that school. I don't have a kid in any school. I guess it's really not my business what happens."

"Sarah, you felt such a sense of pride when you got your certification to become a sommelier. And you're an excellent sommelier. You're very knowledgeable, and you're so helpful to me. You've stocked my wine cellar with some of the best wines worldwide. You have a passion for it and a talent. You're not useless."

Sarah smiled, but Ava could tell that it wasn't a genuine smile. "I know. It's just that I don't have an outlet for my wine talents during the off-season. I don't know, I'm feeling sorry for myself. And I can't let other people's words hurt me so much."

Ava put her arm around her sister. "Sarah, you need to find the young girl who was so confident that she ruled the school. And you definitely need to go forward with your plan to run for school board. You have a very focused vision for how you want the kids in Emerson's school to be. You've talked so much to Emerson about what she thinks is wrong with her school, and that young girl wants your help. Her own mother can't take the time to run for school board or even go to school board meetings, so you have to go in Quinn's stead. Think of Emerson as your child, too. In fact, Emerson is kind of all of our child. It takes a village to raise a child. That village is me, you, and Hallie, along with Quinn."

"So, I guess I'm part of Emerson's village, which means I have a dog in the fight. Is that what you're saying?" Sarah asked her.

"That's what I'm saying."

Sarah took a deep breath, and then the doorbell rang.

Ava shrugged her shoulders. "I wasn't expecting anybody to check in today, but maybe it's a walk-in. Let me check who's there, and as soon as I get them taken care of, we can devise a game plan for you. Because I really want you to pursue the school board thing."

"Okay."

Ava walked to the door and opened it up.

And almost fainted dead away.

Her ex-husband, Christopher, was standing on her porch.

Grab your copy...
vinci-books.com/beachfront-girls